WHAT KATY DID NEXT

by

SUSAN M. COOLIDGE

THE CHILDREN'S PRESS

LONDON AND GLASGOW

This Impression 1976

ISBN 0 00 166024 1

PRINTED AND MADE IN GREAT BRITAIN

CONTENTS

CHAPTER I

THE UNEXPECTED GUEST

THE September sun was glinting cheerfully into a pretty bedroom furnished with blue. It danced on the glossy hair and bright eyes of two girls, who sat together hemming ruffles for a white muslin dress. The half-finished skirt of the dress lay on the bed; and as each crisp ruffle was completed, the girls added it to the snowy heap, which looked like a drift of transparent clouds or a pile of foamy white-of-egg beaten stiff enough to stand alone.

These girls were Clover and Elsie Carr; and it was Clover's first evening dress for which they were hemming ruffles. It was more than three years since Clover and Katy had returned home from the boarding-school at Hillsover.

Clover was now eighteen. She was a very small Clover still, but it would have been hard to find anywhere a prettier little maiden than she had grown to be. Her skin was so exquisitely fair that her arms and wrists and shoulders seemed cut out of daisies or white rose leaves. Her thick, brown hair waved and coiled gracefully about her head. Her smile was peculiarly sweet; and the eyes, always Clover's chief beauty, had still that pathetic look which made them irresistible to tender-hearted people.

Elsie, who adored Clover, considered her as beautiful as girls in books, and was proud to be permitted to hem ruffles for the dress in which she was to burst upon the world. Though, as for that, not much " bursting " was possible in Burnet, where tea-parties of a middle-aged description, and now and then a mild little dance, represented " gaiety " and " society." Girls " came out " by slow degrees and gradual approaches, with no particular one moment which could be fixed upon as having been the crisis of the joyful event.

" There," said Elsie, adding another ruffle to the pile on the bed—" there's the fifth done. It's going to be ever so pretty,

I think. I'm glad you had it all white ; it's a great deal nicer."

" Cecy tried to persuade me to get a long spray of pink roses for the skirt," said Clover.

" I'm so glad you didn't ! Cecy was always crazy about pink roses. I only wonder she didn't wear them when she was married ! "

Yes ; the excellent Cecy, who at thirteen had announced her intention to devote her whole life to teaching Sunday School, visiting the poor, and setting a good example to her more worldly contemporaries, had actually forgotten these fine resolutions, and before she was twenty had become the wife of Sylvester Slack, a young lawyer in a neighbouring town ! Cecy's wedding had been the great excitement of the preceding year in Burnet ; and a fresh excitement had come since in the shape of Cecy's baby, now about two months old, and named " Katherine Clover," after her two friends. Johnnie, at the time we write of, was making her a week's visit.

" She *was* rather wedded to them," went on Clover, pursuing the subject of the pink roses. " She was almost vexed when I wouldn't buy the spray. But it cost lots ; and I didn't want it in the least, so I stood firm. Besides, I always said that my first party dress should be plain white. Girls in novels always wear white to their first balls ; and fresh flowers are a great deal prettier, anyway, than artificial. Katy says she'll give me some violets to wear."

" Oh, will she ? That will be lovely ! " cried the adoring Elsie. " Violets look just like you, somehow."

Just then the noise of someone running upstairs quickly made the sisters look up from their work.

Another moment, the door opened, and Katy dashed in calling out, " Papa !—Elsie, Clover, where's papa ? "

" He went over the river to see that son of Mr. White's who broke his leg. Why, what's the matter ? " asked Clover.

" Is someone hurt ? " inquired Elsie, startled at Katy's agitated looks.

" No, not hurt ; but poor Mrs. Ashe is in such trouble ! "

Mrs. Ashe, it should be explained, was a widow who had come to Burnet some months previously, and had taken a pleasant house not far from the Carrs'. She was a pretty, ladylike woman with a particularly graceful, appealing manner, and very fond of her one child, a little girl. Katy and papa both took a fancy to her at once; and the families had grown neighbourly and intimate in a short time.

" I'll tell you all about it in a minute," went on Katy. " But first I must find Alexander, and send him off to meet papa and beg him to hurry home." She went to the head of the stairs as she spoke, and called " Debby ! " Katy gave her direction, and then came back again to the room where the other two were sitting. " I must explain as fast as I can, for I have got to go back. You know that Mrs. Ashe's little nephew is here for a visit, don't you ? "

" Yes, he came on Saturday."

" Well, he was ailing all day yesterday, and to-day he is worse, and she is afraid it is scarlet fever. Luckily, Amy was spending the day with the Uphams yesterday, so she scarcely saw the boy at all ; and as soon as her mother became alarmed, she sent her out into the garden to play, and hasn't let her come indoors since, so she can't have been exposed to any particular danger yet. I went by the house on my way down the street, and there sat the poor little thing all alone in the garden, with her dolly in her lap, looking so disconsolate. I spoke to her over the fence, and Mrs. Ashe heard my voice, and opened the window and called to me. She said Amy had never had the fever, and that the very idea of her having it frightened her to death. She is such a delicate child, you know."

" Oh, poor Mrs. Ashe ! " cried Clover ; " I am so sorry for her ! Well, Katy, what did you do ? "

" I hope I didn't do wrong, but I offered to bring Amy here. Papa won't object, I am almost sure."

" Why, of course he won't. Well ? "

" I am going back now to fetch Amy. Mrs. Ashe is to let Ellen, who hasn't been in the room with the little boy, pack a bagful of clothes and put it out on the steps, and I shall send Alexander for it by and by. You can't think how troubled poor Mrs. Ashe was. She couldn't help crying when she said that Amy was all she had left in the world. She was so relieved when I said that we would take Amy. You know she has a great deal of confidence in papa."

"Yes, and in you too. Where will you put Amy to sleep, Katy?"

"What do you think would be best? In Dorry's room?"

"I think she'd better come in here with you, and I'll go into Dorry's room. She is used to sleeping with her mother, you know, and she would be lonely if she were left to herself."

"Perhaps that will be better, only it is a great bother for you, Clovy dear."

"I don't mind," responded Clover cheerfully. "I rather like to change about and try a new room once in a while. It's as good as going on a journey—almost."

She pushed aside the half-finished dress as she spoke, opened a drawer, took out its contents, and began to carry them across the entry to Dorry's room, doing everything with the orderly deliberation that was characteristic of whatever Clover did. Her preparations were almost complete before Katy returned, bringing with her little Amy Ashe.

Amy was a tall child of eight, with a frank, happy face, and long light hair hanging down her back. She looked like the pictures of *Alice in Wonderland*; but just at that moment it was a very woeful little Alice indeed that she resembled, for her cheeks were stained with tears and her eyes swollen with recent crying.

"Why, what is the matter?" said Clover. "Aren't you glad that you are coming to us? We are."

"Mamma didn't kiss me for good-bye," sobbed the little girl. "She didn't come downstairs at all. She just put her head out of the window and said: 'Good-bye, Amy! Be very good, and don't make Miss Carr any trouble,' and then she went away. I never went anywhere before without kissing mamma for good-bye."

"Mamma was afraid to kiss you for fear she might give you the fever," explained Katy, taking her turn as a comforter. "It wasn't because she forgot. She felt worse about it than you did, I imagine. You know the thing she cares for most is that you shall not be ill as your cousin Walter is. She would rather do anything than have that happen. As soon as he gets well she will kiss you dozens of times, see if she doesn't. Meanwhile, she says in this note that you must write her a little letter every day, and she will hang a basket by a string out of the window, and you and I will go and drop the letters into the basket, and stand by the gate and see her pull it up. That will be funny, won't it ? "

" Shall I sleep with you ? " demanded Amy.

" Yes, in that bed over there."

" It's a pretty bed," pronounced Amy after examining it gravely for a moment. " Will you tell me a story every morning ? "

" If you don't wake up too early. My stories are always sleepy till seven o'clock. Let us see what Ellen has packed and then I'll give you some drawers of your own, and we will put the things away."

The bag was full of neat little frocks and underclothes stuffed hastily in all together. Katy took them out, smoothing the folds with her fingers. As she lifted the last skirt, Amy, with a cry of joy, pounced on something that lay beneath it.

" It's Maria Matilda," she said ; " I'm glad of that. I thought Ellen would forget her, and the poor child wouldn't know what to do."

" What a pretty face she has ! " said Katy, taking the doll out of Amy's hands.

" Yes, but not so pretty as Mabel. Miss Upham says that Mabel is the prettiest child she ever saw. Look, Miss Clover," lifting the other doll from the table where she had laid it, " hasn't she got *sweet* eyes ? She's older than Maria Matilda, and she knows a great deal more. She's begun on French verbs ! "

" Not really ! Which ones ? "

" Oh, only ' J'aime, tu aimes, il aime,' you know—the same one that our class is learning at school. She hasn't tried any but that. Sometimes she says it quite nicely, but sometimes she's very stupid, and I have to scold her." Amy had quite recovered her spirits by this time.

" Are these the only dolls you have ? "

" Oh, please don't call them that ! " urged Amy. " It hurts their feelings dreadfully. I never let them know that they are dolls. They think that they are real children, only sometimes, when they are very bad, I use the word for a punishment. I've got several other children. There's old Ragazza. My uncle named her, and she's made of rag, but she has such bad rheumatism that I don't play with her any longer ; I just give her medicine. Then there's Effie Deans, she's only got one leg ; and Mopsa the Fairy, she's a tiny one made out of china ; and Peg of Linkinvaddy—but she don't count, for she's come all to pieces."

" What very queer names your children have ! " said Elsie, who had come in during the enumeration.

" Yes ; Uncle Ned named them. He's a very funny uncle, but he's nice. He's always so much interested in my children."

" There's papa now ! " cried Katy ; and she ran downstairs to meet him.

" Did I do right ? " she asked anxiously, after she had told her story.

" Yes, my dear, perfectly right," replied Dr. Carr. " I only hope Amy was taken away in time. I will go round at once to see Mrs. Ashe and the boy ; and, Katy, keep away from me when I come back and keep the others away, till I have changed my coat."

It seemed to the Carrs after a few days as if they had always had Amy in the house with them. Papa's daily visit to the sickroom, their avoidance of him till after he had " changed his coat," Amy's lessons and games, her dressing and undressing, the walks, and the dropping of notes into the little basket, seemed part of the system of things which had been going on for a long time, and which everybody would miss should they suddenly stop.

But they by no means suddenly stopped. Little Walter Ashe's case proved to be a rather severe one ; and after he had begun to mend, he caught cold somehow and was taken worse again. There were some serious symptoms, and for a few days Dr. Carr did not feel sure how things would turn. He did not speak of his anxiety at home, but kept silence and a cheerful face, as doctors know how to do. Only Katy, who was more intimate with her father than the rest, guessed that things were going gravely at the other house, and she was too well trained to ask questions. The threatening symptoms passed off, however, and little Walter slowly got better ; but it was a long convalescence, and Mrs. Ashe grew thin and pale, before he began to look rosy. There was no one on whom she could devolve the charge of the child. His mother was dead ; his father, an over-worked business man, had barely time to run up once a week to see about him : there was no one at his home but a house-keeper, in whom Mrs. Ashe had not full confidence. So the good aunt denied herself the sight of her own child, and devoted her strength and time to Walter, and nearly two months passed, and still little Amy remained at Dr. Carr's.

She was entirely happy there. She had grown very fond of Katy, and was perfectly at home with the others. Phil and Johnnie, who had returned from her visit to Cecy, were by no means too old or too proud to be play-fellows to a child of eight ; and with all the older members of the family Amy was a chosen pet. Debby baked turnovers, and twisted cinnamon cakes into all sorts of fantastic shapes to please her ; Alexander would let her drive if she happened to sit on the front seat of the carry-all ; Dr. Carr was seldom so tired that he could not tell her a story ; Elsie invented all manner of charming games for the hour before bedtime ; Clover made wonderful capes and bonnets for Mabel and Maria Matilda ; and Katy—Katy did all sorts of things.

Katy had a peculiar gift with children which is not easy to define. Some people possess it, and some do not ; it cannot be learned, it comes by nature. She was bright and firm and equable all at once. She both amused and influenced them. There was something about her which excited the childish imagination, and always they felt her sympathy. Amy was a tractable child, and intelligent beyond her age, but she was never quite so good with anyone as with Katy. She followed her about like a little lover ; she lavished upon her certain special words and caresses which she gave to no one else ; and would kneel on her lap, patting Katy's shoulders with her soft hand, and cooing up into her face like a happy dove, for a half-hour together. Katy laughed at these demonstrations, but they pleased her very much.

At last, the long convalescence ended, Walter was carried away by his father, and an army of work-people was turned into Mrs. Ashe's house. Plaster was scraped and painted, wall-papers torn down, mattresses made over, and clothing burned. At last

Dr. Carr pronounced the premises in a sanitary condition, and Mrs. Ashe sent for her little girl to come home.

Amy was overjoyed at the prospect of seeing her mother ; but at the last moment she clung to Katy and cried as if her heart would break.

" I want you too," she said. " Oh, if Dr. Carr would only let you come and live with me and mamma, I should be so happy ! I shall be so lone-ly ! "

" Nonsense ! " cried Clover. " Lonely with mamma, and those poor children of yours who have been wondering all these weeks what has become of you ! They'll want a great deal of attention at first, I am sure ; medicine and new clothes and whippings—all manner of things. You remember I promised to make a dress for Effie Deans out of that blue-and-brown plaid like Johnnie's balmoral. I mean to begin it to-morrow."

" Oh, will you ? "—forgetting her grief—" Lovely. She will be so pleased, for she's never had a new dress." Consoled by the prospect of Effie's satisfaction, Amy departed quite cheerfully, and Mrs. Ashe was spared the pain of seeing her only child in tears on the first evening of their reunion. But Amy talked so constantly of Katy, and seemed to love her so much, that it put a plan into her mother's head which led to important results.

CHAPTER II

AN INVITATION

IT IS a curious fact that, generally speaking, none of us have any expectation that things are going to happen till the very moment when they do happen. We wake up some morning with no idea that a great happiness is at hand and before night it has come, and all the world is changed for us ; or we wake bright and cheerful, with never a guess that clouds of sorrow are lowering in our sky, and before noon all is dark. Nothing whispers of either the joy or the grief.

Nothing whispered to Katy Carr, as she sat at the window mending a long rent in Johnnie's school coat, and saw Mrs. Ashe come in at the side gate and ring the office bell, that the visit had any special significance for her. Mrs. Ashe often did come to the office to consult Dr. Carr. Amy might not be quite well, Katy thought, or there might be a letter with something about Walter in it, or perhaps matters had gone wrong at the house, where paperers and painters were still at work. So she went calmly on with her darning, drawing the " ravelling," with which her needle was threaded, carefully in and out and taking nice even stitches without one prophetic thrill or tremor, while, if only she could have heard what Mrs. Ashe was saying, the school coat would have been thrown to the winds, and for all her tall stature and propriety she would have been skipping with delight and astonishment. For Mrs. Ashe was asking papa to let her do the very thing of all others that she most longed to do ; she was asking him to let Katy go with her to Europe !

" I am not very well," she told the Doctor. " I got tired and run down while Walter was ill, and I don't seem to throw it off as I hoped I should. I feel as if a change would do me good. Don't you think so yourself ? "

" Yes, I do," Dr. Carr admitted.

" This idea of Europe is not altogether a new one," continued Mrs. Ashe. " I have always meant to go sometime, and have put it off, partly because I dreaded going alone, and didn't know anybody whom I wanted to take with me. But if you will let me have Katy, Dr. Carr, it will settle all my difficulties. Amy loves her dearly, and so do I ; she is just the companion I need ; if I have her with me, I shan't be afraid of anything."

" How long do you mean to be away ? " asked Dr. Carr, divided between pleasure at these compliments to Katy and dismay at the idea of losing her.

" About a year, I think. My plans are rather vague as yet ; but my idea was to spend a few weeks in Scotland and England first—I have some cousins in London who will be good to us ; and an old friend of mine married a gentleman who lives on the Isle of Wight ; perhaps we might go there. Then we could cross over to France, and visit Paris ; and before it gets cold, go down to Nice, and from there to Italy.

" There is one reason why I thought Italy would be particularly pleasant this winter for me," went on Mrs. Ashe ; " and that is, because my brother will be there. He is a lieutenant in the navy, you know, and his ship, the *Natchitoches*, is one of the Mediterranean squadron. They will be in Naples by and by, and if we were there at the same time we should have Ned to go about with ; and he would take us to the receptions on the frigate, and all that, which would be a nice chance for Katy. Then towards spring I should like to go to Florence and Venice, and visit the Italian lakes and Switzerland in the early summer. But all this depends on your letting Katy go. If you decide against it, I shall give the whole thing up. But you won't decide against it "—coaxingly—" you will be kinder than that. I will take the best possible care of her, and do all I can to make her happy, if only you will consent to lend her to me ; and I shall consider it *such* a favour. And it is to cost you nothing. You understand, Doctor, she is to be my guest all through. I want to make that clear in the outset ; for she goes for my sake, and I cannot take her on any other conditions. Now, Dr. Carr, please ! I am sure you won't deny me, when I have so set my heart upon having her."

Mrs. Ashe was very pretty and persuasive, but still Dr. Carr hesitated. To send Katy for a year's pleasuring in Europe was a thing that had never occurred to his mind as possible. The cost alone would have prevented, for country doctors with six children are not apt to be rich men. It seemed equally impossible to let her go at Mrs. Ashe's expense ; at the same time, the chance was such a good one, and Mrs. Ashe so much in earnest and so urgent, that it was difficult to refuse point-blank. He finally consented to take time for consideration before making his decision.

" I will talk it over with Katy," he said. " The child ought to have a say in the matter ; and whatever we decide, you must let me thank you in her name as well as my own for your great kindness in proposing it."

" Doctor, I'm not kind at all, and I don't want to be thanked. My desire to take Katy with me to Europe is purely selfish. I am a lonely person," she went on ; " I have no mother or sister, and my brother's profession keeps him at sea ; I scarcely ever see him. I have no one but a couple of old aunts, too feeble in health to travel with me or to be counted on in case of any emergency. You see, I am a real case for pity."

Mrs. Ashe spoke gaily, but her brown eyes were dim with tears as she ended her little appeal. Dr. Carr, who was soft-hearted where women were concerned, was touched. Perhaps his face showed it, for Mrs. Ashe added in a more hopeful tone :

" But I won't tease any more. I know you will not refuse me unless you think it right and necessary ; and," she continued mischievously, " I have great faith in Katy as an ally. I am pretty sure that she will say that she wants to go."

And indeed Katy's cry of delight when the plan was proposed to her said that sufficiently, without need of further explanation. To go to Europe for a year with Mrs. Ashe and Amy seemed simply too delightful to be true. All the things she had heard about and read about came rushing into her mind. Dr. Carr's objections, his reluctance to part with her, melted before the radiance of her satisfaction. He had no idea that Katy would care so much about it. After all, it was a great chance—per-haps the only one of the sort that she would ever have. Mrs. Ashe could well afford to give Katy this treat, he knew, and it was quite true what she said, that it was a favour to her as well as to Katy. This train of reasoning led to its natural results. Dr. Carr began to waver in his mind.

But, the first excitement over, Katy's second thoughts were more sober ones. How could papa manage without her for a whole year, she asked herself. He would miss her, she well knew ; and might not the charge of the house be too much for Clover ? A host of housewifely cares began to troop through Katy's mind, a little pucker came into her forehead, and a wor-ried look across the face which had been so bright a few minutes before.

Strange to say, it was that little pucker and the look of worry which decided Dr. Carr.

" She is only twenty-one," he reflected ; " hardly out of childhood. I don't want her to settle into an anxious drudging state, and lose her youth with caring for us all. She shall go ; though how we are to manage without her I don't see. Little

Clover will have to come to the fore, and show what sort of stuff there is in her."

Little Clover came gallantly " to the fore " when the first shock of surprise was over, and she had relieved her mind with one long private cry over having to do without Katy for a year. Then she wiped her eyes, and began to revel unselfishly in the idea of her sister's having so great a treat. Anything and everything seemed possible to secure it for her ; and she made light of all Katy's many anxieties and apprehensions.

" My dear child, I know a flannel undershirt when I see one, just as well as you do," she declared. " Tucks in Johnnie's dress, forsooth ! Ripping out a tuck doesn't require any super-human ingenuity ! Quince marmalade ? Debby can make that. Hers is about as good as yours ; and if it wasn't, what should we care, as long as you are ascending Mont Blanc, and hob-nobbing with Michael Angelo and the crowned heads of Europe ? I'll make the spiced peaches ! I'll order the kindling ! And if there ever comes a time when I feel lost and can't manage with-out advice, I'll go across to Mrs. Hall. Don't worry about us. We shall get on happily and easily ; in fact, I shouldn't be sur-prised if I develop such a turn for housekeeping, that when you come back the family refused to change, and you had just to sit for the rest of your life and twirl your thumbs ! Wouldn't that be fine ? " and Clover laughed merrily. " So, Katy darling, cast that shadow from your brow, and look as a girl ought to look who's going to Europe. Why, if it were I who were going, I should simply stand on my head every moment of the time ! "

" Not a very convenient position for packing," said Katy, smiling.

" Yes, it is if you turn your trunk upside down ! When I think of all the delightful things you are going to do I can hardly sit still. I *love* Mrs. Ashe for inviting you."

" So do I," said Katy soberly. " It was the kindest thing. I can't think why she did it."

" Well, I can," replied Clover, always ready to defend Katy even against herself. " She did it because she wanted you, and she wanted you because you are the dearest old thing in the world, and the nicest to have about. You needn't say you're

not, for you are ! Now, Katy, don't waste another thought on such miserable things as pickles and undershirts. We shall get along perfectly well, I do assure you. Just fix your mind instead on the dome of St. Peter's, or try to fancy how you'll feel the first time you step into a gondola or see the Mediterranean. There will be a moment ! What fun it will be to get your letters ! We shall fetch out the Encyclopædia and the big Atlas and the *History of Modern Europe*, and read all about everything you see and all the places you go to ; and it will be as good as a lesson in geography and history and political economy all combined, only a great deal more interesting ! We shall stick out all over with knowledge before you come back ; and this makes it a plain duty to go, if it were only for our sakes."
With these zealous promises, Katy was forced to be content. Indeed, contentment was not difficult with such a prospect of delight before her. When once her little anxieties had been laid aside, the idea of the coming journey grew in pleasantness every moment.

Katy learned a great deal while talking over what she was to see and do. She read every scrap she could lay her hand on which related to Rome or Florence or Venice or London. The driest details had a charm for her now that she was likely to see the real places. She went about with scraps of paper in her pocket, on which were written such things as these : " Forum. When built ? By whom built ? More than one ? " " What does *Cenacola* mean ? " " Cecilia Metella. Who was she ? " " Find out about Saint Catherine of Siena." " Who was Beatrice Cenci ? " How she wished that she had studied harder and more carefully before this wonderful chance came to her !

All Burnet took an interest in Katy's plans, and almost everybody had some sort of advice or help, or some little gift to offer. Old Mrs. Worrett, who, though fatter than ever, still retained the power of locomotion, drove in from Conic Section in her roomy carry-all with the present of a rather obsolete copy of *Murray's Guide*, in faded red covers, which her father had used in his youth, also a bottle of Brown's Jamaica Ginger, in case of sea-sickness. Debby's sister-in-law brought a bundle of dried camomile for the same purpose. Someone had told her it was the " handiest thing in the world to take along with you on them steamboats." Cecy sent a wonderful old-gold and scarlet contrivance to hang on the wall of the state-room. There were pockets for watches, and pockets for medicines, and pockets for handkerchiefs and hairpins—in short, there were pockets for everything; besides a pin-cushion with "Bon Voyage" in rows of shining pins, a bottle of eau-de-Cologne, a cake of soap, and a hammer and tacks to nail the whole up with. Mrs. Hall's gift was a warm and very pretty woollen wrapper of dark blue flannel, with a pair of soft-knitted slippers to match. Old Mr. Worrett sent a note of advice, recommending Katy to take a quinine pill every day that she was away, never to stay out late, because the dews "over there" were said to be unwholesome, and on no account to drink a drop of water which had not been boiled.

From Cousin Helen came a delightful travelling-bag, light and strong at once, and fitted up with all manner of nice little conveniences. Miss Inches sent a *History of Europe* in five fat volumes, which was so heavy that it had to be left at home. In fact, a good many of Katy's presents had to be left at home, for both Mrs. Ashe and Cousin Helen had warned her of the inconvenient consequences of weight in baggage : and by their advice she had limited herself to a single trunk of moderate size, besides a little flat valise for use in her state-room.

Clover's gift was a set of blank books for notes, journals, etc. In one of these Katy made out a list of "Things I must see," "Things I must do," "Things I would like to see," "Things I would like to do." Another she devoted to various good shopping addresses which had been given her ; for though she did not expect to do any shopping herself, she thought Mrs. Ashe might find them useful. Katy's ideas were still so simple and unworldly, and her experience of life so small, that it had not occurred to her how very tantalising it might be to stand in front of shop windows full of delightful things and not be able to buy any of them. She was accordingly overpowered with surprise, gratitude, and the sense of sudden wealth, when, about a week before the start, her father gave her three little thin strips of paper, which he told her were circular notes, and worth a hundred dollars apiece. He also gave her five English sovereigns.

" Those are for immediate use," he said. " Put the notes away carefully, and don't lose them. You had better have them cashed one at a time as you require them. Mrs. Ashe will explain how. You will need a gown or so before you come back, and you'll want to buy some photographs and so on, and there will be fees——"

" But, Papa," protested Katy, opening wide her candid eyes, " I didn't expect you to give me any money, and I'm afraid you are giving me too much. Do you think you can afford it? Really and truly, I don't want to buy things. I shall see everything, you know, and that's enough."

Her father only laughed.

" You'll be wiser and greedier before the year is out, my dear," he replied. " Three hundred dollars won't go far, as you'll find. But it's all I can spare, and I trust you to keep within it, and not come home with any long bills for me to pay."

" Papa! I should think not!" cried Katy, with unsophisticated horror.

One very interesting thing was to happen before they sailed, the thought of which helped both Katy and Clover through the last hard days, when the preparations were nearly complete, and the family had leisure to feel dull and out of spirits. Katy was to make Rose Red a visit.

Rose had by no means been idle during the three years and a half which had elapsed since they all parted at Hillsover, and during which the girls had not seen her. In fact, she had made more out of the time than any of the rest of them, for she had been engaged for eighteen months, had been married, and was now keeping house near Boston with a little Rose of her own, who, she wrote to Clover, was a perfect angel, and more delicious than words could say! Mrs. Ashe had taken passage in the *Spartacus*, sailing from Boston; and it was arranged that Katy should spend the last two days before sailing with Rose, while Mrs. Ashe and Amy visited an old aunt in Hingham. To see Rose in her own home, and Rose's husband, and Rose's baby, was only next in interest to seeing Europe. None of the changes in her lot seemed to have changed her particularly, to judge by the letter she sent in reply to Katy's announcing her plans, which letter ran as follows :

Longwood,
September 20th

" MY DEAREST CHILD,

" Your note made me dance with delight. I stood on my head, waving my heels wildly to the breeze, till Deniston thought I must be taken suddenly mad ; but when I explained he did the same. It is too enchanting, the whole of it. I put it at the head of all the nice things that ever happened, except my baby. Write the moment you get this by what train you expect to reach Boston, and when you roll into the station you will behold two forms, one tall and stalwart, the other short and fatsome, waiting for you. They will be those of Deniston and myself. Deniston is not beautiful, but he is good, and he is prepared to *adore* you. The baby is both good and beautiful, and you will adore her. I am neither ; but you know all about me, and I always did adore you and always shall. I am going out this moment to the butcher's to order a calf fatted for your special behoof ; and he shall be slain and made into cutlets the moment I hear from you. My funny little house, which is quite a dear little house too, assumes a new interest in my eyes from the fact that you so soon are to see it. It is somewhat queer, as you might know my house would be ; but I think you will like it.

" I saw Silvery Mary the other day and told her you were coming. She is the same mouse as ever. I shall ask her and some of the other girls to come out to lunch on one of your days. Good-bye, with a hundred and fifty kisses to Clovy and the rest.

" Your loving
" ROSE RED."

" She never signs herself Browne, I observe," said Clover, as she finished the letter.

" Oh, Rose Red Browne would sound too funny ! Rose Red she must stay till the end of the chapter ; no other name could suit her half so well, and I can't imagine her being called anything else. What fun it will be to see her and little Rose ! "

" And Deniston Browne," put in Clover.

" Somehow I find it rather hard to take in the fact that there is a Deniston Browne," observed Katy.

" It will be easier after you have seen him, perhaps."

The last day came, as last days will. Katy's trunk, most carefully and exactly packed by the united efforts of the family, stood in the hall, locked and strapped, not to be opened again till the party reached London. The little valise was also ready ; and Dorry, the neat-handed, had painted a red star on both ends of both it and the trunk, that they might be easily picked from among a heap of luggage. He now proceeded to prepare and paste on two square cards, labelled respectively, " Hold " and " State-room." Mrs. Hall had told them that this was the correct thing to do.

Mrs. Ashe had been full of business likewise in putting her house to rights for a family who had rented it for the time of her absence, and Katy and Clover had taken a good many hours from their own preparations to help her. All was done at last ; and one bright morning in October, Katy stood on the wharf with her family about her, and a lump in her throat which made it difficult to speak. She stood so very still, and said so very little, that a bystander not acquainted with the circumstances might have dubbed her " unfeeling "; while the fact was that she was feeling too much !

The first bell rang. Katy kissed everybody quietly and went on board with her father. Her parting from him, hardest of all, took place in the midst of a crowd of people ; then he had to leave her, and as the wheels began to revolve she went out on the side deck to have a last glimpse of the home faces. There they were : Elsie crying tumultuously, with her head on papa's coat-sleeve ; John laughing, or trying to laugh, with big tears running down her cheeks the while ; and brave little Clover waving her handkerchief encouragingly, but with a very sober look on her face. Katy's heart went out to the little group with a sudden passion of regret and yearning. Why had she said she would go ? What was all Europe in comparison with what she was leaving ? Life was so short, how could she take a whole year out of it to spend away from the people she loved best ? If it had been left to her to choose, I think she would have fiown back to the shore then and there, and given up the journey.

I also think she would have been heartily sorry a little later, had she done so.

But it was not left for her to choose. Already the throb of the engines was growing more regular and the distance widening between the great boat and the wharf. Gradually the dear faces faded into distance ; and Katy went to the cabin with a heavy heart. But there were Mrs. Ashe and Amy, inclined to be home-sick also, and in need of cheering, and Katy, as she tried to brighten them, gradually grew bright herself, and recovered her hopeful spirits. Burnet pulled less strongly as it got farther away, and Europe beckoned more brilliantly now that they were fairly embarked on their journey. The sun shone, the lake was a beautiful, dazzling blue, and Katy said to herself : " After all, a year is not very long, and how happy I am going to be ! "

CHAPTER III

ROSE AND ROSEBUD

THIRTY-SIX hours later the Albany train brought the travellers to Boston.

Katy looked eagerly from the window for her first glimpse of the city of which she had heard so much. After flat Burnet, with its one bank down to the edge of the lake, it looked large, imposing, and very picturesque. She studied the towers, steeples, and red roofs crowding each other up the slopes of the Tri-Mountain, and the big State House dome crowning all, and made up her mind that she liked the looks of it better than any other city she had ever seen.

The train slackened its speed, ran for a few moments between rows of tall, shabby brick walls, and with a long, final screech of its whistle came to halt in the station-house. Everyone made a simultaneous rush for the door ; and Katy and Mrs. Ashe, waiting to collect their books and bags, found themselves wedged into their seats and unable to get out.

But the discomfort brightened into a sense of relief as, looking out of the window, Katy caught sight of a face exactly opposite, which had evidently caught sight of her—a fresh, pretty face, with light, waving hair, pink cheeks all a-dimple, and eyes which shone with laughter and welcome. It was Rose herself, not a bit changed during the years since they parted. A tall young man stood beside her, who must, of course, be her husband, Deniston Browne.

"There is Rose Red," cried Katy to Mrs. Ashe. "Oh, doesn't she look dear and natural? Do wait and let me introduce you. I want you to know her."

But the train had come in a little behind time, and Mrs. Ashe was afraid of missing the Hingham boat; so she only took a hasty peep from the window at Rose, pronounced her to be charming-looking, kissed Katy hurriedly, reminded her that they must be on the steamer at twelve o'clock the following Saturday, and was gone, so that Katy, following last of all the slow-moving line of passengers, stepped all alone down from the platform into the arms of Rose Red.

"You darling!" was Rose's first greeting. "I began to think you meant to spend the night in the car, you were so long getting out. Well, how lovely this is! Deniston, here is Katy; Katy, this is my husband."

Rose looked about fifteen as she spoke, and so absurdly young to have a husband, that Katy could not help laughing as she shook hands with Deniston, and his own eyes twinkled with fun and evident recognition of the same joke. He was a tall young man, with a pleasant, "steady" face, and seemed to be amused, in a quiet way, with everything which his wife said and did.

"Let us make haste and get out of this hole," went on Rose. "I can scarcely see for the smoke. Deniston, dear, please find a cab, and have Katy's luggage put on it. I am wild to get her home, and exhibit baby before she chews up her new sash or does something else that is dreadful, to spoil her looks. I left her sitting in state, Katy, with all her best clothes on, waiting to be made known to you."

"My large trunk is to go straight to the steamer," explained Katy, as she gave her checks to Mr. Browne. "I only want the little one taken out to Longwood, please."

"Now, this is cosy," remarked Rose, when they were seated

in the cab with Katy's bag at their feet. " Deniston, my love, I wish you were going out with us. There's a nice little bench here all ready and vacant, which is just suited to a man of your inches. You won't ? Well, come in the early train, then. Don't forget. Now, isn't he just as nice as I told you he was ? " she demanded, the moment the cab began to move.

" He looks very nice indeed, as far as I can judge in three minutes and a quarter."

" My dear, it ought not to take anybody of ordinary discernment a minute and a quarter to perceive that he is simply the dearest fellow that ever lived," said Rose. " I discovered it three seconds after I first beheld him, and was desperately in love with him before he had fairly finished his first bow after introduction."

" And was he equally prompt ? " asked Katy.

" He says so," replied Rose, with a pretty blush. " But then he could hardly say less after such a frank confession on my part. It is no more than decent of him to make me believe, even if it is not true. Now, Katy, look at Boston, and see if you don't *love* it ! "

Rose was quite satisfied with her raptures as they drove through Charles Street, between the Common and the Public Garden, all ablaze with autumn flowers, and down the length of Beacon Street with the blue bay shining between the handsome houses on the water-side. Every vestibule and bay-window was gay with potted plants and flower-boxes ; and a concourse of happy-looking people, on foot, on horseback, and in carriages, was surging to and fro like an equal, prosperous tide, while the sunlight glorified all.

" ' Boston shows a soft Venetian side '," quoted Katy, after a while. " I know now what Mr. Lowell meant when he wrote that. I don't believe there is a more beautiful place in the world."

" Why of course there isn't," retorted Rose, who was a most devoted little Bostonian, in spite of the fact that she had lived in Washington nearly all her life. " I've not seen much beside, to be sure, but that is no matter ; I know it is true. It is the dream of my life to come into the city to live. I don't care what part I live in, so long as it is Boston ! "

"But don't you like Longwood?" asked Katy, looking out admiringly at the pretty places set amid vines and shrubberies which they were now passing. "It looks so very pretty and pleasant."

"Yes, it's well enough for anyone who has a taste for natural beauties," replied Rose. "I haven't; I never had. There is nothing I hate so much as Nature! I'm a born cockney. I'd rather live in one room over Jordan and Marsh's, and see the world wag past, than be the owner of the most romantic villa that ever was built."

The cab now turned in at a gate and followed a curving drive bordered with trees to a pretty stone house with a porch embowered with Virginia creepers, before which it stopped.

"Here we are!" cried Rose, springing out. "Now, Katy, you mustn't even take time to sit down before I show you the dearest baby that ever was sent to this sinful earth. Here, let me take your bag; come straight upstairs, and I will exhibit her to you."

They ran up accordingly, and Rose took Katy into a large sunny nursery, where, tied with pink ribbons into a little basket-chair and watched over by a pretty young nurse, sat a dear, fat, fair baby, so exactly like Rose that no one could possibly have mistaken the relationship. The baby began to laugh and coo as soon as it caught sight of its gay little mother and exhibited just such another dimple as hers in the middle of a pink cheek. Katy was enchanted.

"Oh, you darling!" she said. "Would she come to me, do you think, Rose?"

"Why, of course she shall!" replied Rose, picking up the baby as if she had been a pillow and stuffing her into Katy's arms head first. "Now, just look at her, and tell me if ever you saw anything so enchanting in the whole course of your life before? Isn't she big? Isn't she beautiful? Isn't she good? Just see her little hands and her hair! She never cries except when it is clearly her duty to cry. See her turn her head to look at me! Oh, you angel!" And, seizing the long-suffering baby, she smothered it with kisses. "I never, never, never did see anything so sweet."

Little Rose was indeed a delicious baby, all dimples and good-humour and violet powder, with a skin as soft as a lily's leaf, and a happy capacity for allowing herself to be petted and cuddled without remonstrance. She was so soft and sunny and equable that it was no more trouble to care for and amuse her than if she had been a bird or a kitten ; and, as Rose remarked, it was " ten times better fun."

" I was never allowed as many dolls as I wanted in my infancy," she said. " I suppose I tore them to pieces too soon ; and they couldn't give me tin ones to play with, as they did wash-bowls, when I broke the china ones."

" Were you such a very bad child ? " asked Katy.

" Oh, utterly depraved, I believe ! You wouldn't think so now, would you ? I recollect some dreadful occasions at school. Once I had my head pinned up in my apron because I *would* make faces at the other scholars and they laughed ; but I promptly bit a bay-window through the apron, and ran my tongue out of it till they laughed worse than ever. The teacher used to send me home with notes fastened to my pinafore with things like this written in them : ' Little Frisk has been more troublesome than usual to-day. She has pinched all the younger children, and bent the bonnets of all the older ones. We hope to see an amendment soon, or we do not know what we shall do '."

" Why did they call you Little Frisk ? " inquired Katy, after she had recovered from the laugh which Rose's reminiscences called forth.

" It was a term of endearment, I suppose ; but somehow my family never seemed to enjoy it as they ought. I cannot understand," she went on reflectively, " why I had not sense enough to suppress those awful little notes. It would have been so easy to lose them on the way home, but somehow it never occurred to me. Little Rose will be wiser than that ; won't you, my angel ? She will tear up the horrid notes—mammy will show her how ! "

All the time that Katy was washing her face and brushing the dust of the railway from her dress, Rose sat by with the little Rose in her lap, entertaining her thus. When she was ready, the droll little mamma tucked her baby under her arm and led the way downstairs to a large square parlour with a bay-window, through which the westering sun was shining. It was a pretty room, and had a flavour about it " just like Rose," Katy declared. No one else would have hung the pictures or hooked back the curtains in exactly that way, or have hit upon the happy device of filling the grate with a great bunch of marigolds, pale brown, golden, and orange, to simulate the fire. She had chosen a " greenery, yallery " paper for her walls, against which hung various articles which looked a great deal queerer then than they would to-day. There was a mandolin, picked up at some Eastern sale, a warming-pan in shining brass from her mother's attic, two old samplers worked in faded silks, and a quantity of gaily-tinted Japanese fans and embroideries. She had also begged from an old aunt at Beverly Farms a couple of droll little arm-chairs in white painted wood, with covers of antique needle-work. One had Chit embroidered on the middle of its cushion; the other, Chat.

" Now, Katy," said Rose, seating herself in Chit, " pull up Chat, and let us begin."

So they did begin, and went on, interrupted only by Baby Rose's coos and splutters till the dusk fell, till appetising smells floated through from the rear of the house, and the click of a latch-key announced Mr. Browne, come home just in time for dinner.

The two days' visit went only too quickly. There is nothing more fascinating to a girl than the *ménage* of a young couple of her own age. It is a sort of playing at real life without the cares and the sense of responsibility that real life is sure to bring. Rose was an adventurous housekeeper. She was still new to the position, she found it very entertaining, and she delighted in experiments of all sorts. If they turned out well, it was good fun; if not, that was funnier still ! Her husband, for all his serious manner, had a real boy's love of a lark, and he aided and abetted her in all sorts of whimsical devices. They owned a dog who was only less dear than the baby, a cat only less dear than the dog, a parrot whose education required constant supervision, and a hutch of ring-doves whose melancholy little " whuddering " coos were the delight of Rose. The house seemed astir with young life all over. The only elderly thing in it was the cook, who had the reputation of a dreadful temper;

only, unfortunately, Rose made her laugh so much that she never found time to be cross.

Katy felt quite an old, experienced person amid all this movement and liveliness and cheer. It seemed to her that nobody in the world could possibly be having such a good time as Rose ; but Rose did not take the same view of the situation.

" It's all very well now," she said, " while the warm weather lasts ; but in winter Longwood is simply gruesome. The wind never stops blowing day or night. It howls and it roars and it screams, till I feel as if every nerve in my body were on the point of snapping in two. And the snow, ugh ! And the wind, ugh ! And burglars ! Every night of our lives they come—or I think they come—and I lie awake and hear them sharpening their tools and forcing the locks and murdering the cook and kidnapping Baby, till I long to die and have done with them forever ! Oh, Nature is the most unpleasant thing ! "

" Burglars are not Nature," objected Katy.

" What are they, then ? Art ? High Art ? Well, whatever they are, I do not like them. Oh, if ever the happy day comes when Deniston consents to move into town, I never wish to set my eyes on the country again as long as I live, unless—well, yes, I should like to come out just once more in the horse-cars and *kick* that elm-tree by the fence ! The number of times that I have lain awake at night listening to its creaking ! "

" You might kick it without waiting to have a house in town."

" Oh, I shouldn't dare as long as we are living here ! You never know what Nature may do. She has ways of her own of getting even with people," remarked her friend, solemnly.

No time must be lost in showing Boston to Katy, Rose said. So, the morning after her arrival she was taken in bright and early to see the sights. Then the girls did a little shopping ; and by that time they were quite tired enough to make the idea of luncheon agreeable, so they took the path across the Common to the Joy Street Mall.

Katy was charmed by all she had seen. The delightful nearness of so many interesting things surprised her. She perceived what is one of Boston's chief charms—that the Common and its surrounding streets make a natural centre and rally-point for the whole city. The stately old houses on Beacon Street, with their rounded fronts, deep window-casements, and here and there a mauve or a lilac pane set in the sashes, took her fancy greatly; and so did the State House, whose situation made it sufficiently imposing, even before the gilding of the dome.

Up the steep steps of the Joy Street Mall they went, to the house on Mt. Vernon Street which the Reddings had taken on their return from Washington nearly three years before. Rose had previously shown Katy the site of the old family house on Summer Street, where she was born, now given over wholly to warehouses and shops. Their present residence was one of those wide, old-fashioned brick houses on the crest of the hill, whose upper windows command the view across to the Boston Highlands; in the rear was a spacious yard, almost large enough to be called a garden, walled in with ivies and grape-vines, under which were long beds full of roses and chrysanthemums and marigolds and mignonette.

Rose carried a latch-key in her pocket, which she said had been one of her wedding-gifts; with this she unlocked the front door and let Katy into a roomy white-painted hall.

"We will go straight through to the back steps," she said. "Mamma is sure to be sitting there; she always sits there till the first frost; she says it makes her think of the country."

There, to be sure, Mrs. Redding was found sitting in a wicker-work chair under the shade of the grape-vines, with a big basket of mending at her side. It looked so homely and country-like to find a person thus occupied in the middle of a busy city that Katy's heart warmed to her at once.

Mrs. Redding was a fair little woman, scarcely taller than Rose and very much like her. She gave Katy a kind welcome. "You do not seem like a stranger," she said. "Rose has told us so much about you and your sister. Sylvia will be very disappointed not to see you. She went off to make some visits when we broke up in the country, and is not to be home for three weeks yet."

Katy was disappointed too, for she had heard a great deal about Sylvia and had wished very much to meet her. She was shown her picture, from which she gathered that she did not look in the least like Rose; for, though equally fair, her fairness was of the tall aquiline type, quite different from Rose's dimpled prettiness. In fact, Rose resembled her mother, and Sylvia her father; they were only alike in little peculiarities of voice and manner, of which a portrait did not enable Katy to judge.

The two girls had a cosy little luncheon with Mrs. Redding, after which Rose carried Katy off to see the house and everything in it which was in any way connected with her own personal history—the room where she used to sleep, the high-chair in which she sat as a baby and which was presently to be made over to little Rose, the sofa where Deniston offered himself, and the exact spot on the carpet on which she had stood while they were being married! Last of all——

"Now you shall see the best and dearest thing in the whole house," she said, opening the door of a room in the second story—"Grandmamma, here is my friend Katy Carr, whom you have so often heard me tell about."

It was a large, pleasant room, with a little wood-fire blazing in the grate, by which, in an arm-chair full of cushions, with a solitaire-board on a little table beside her, sat a sweet old lady. This was Rose's father's mother. She was nearly eighty; but she was beautiful still, and her manner had a gracious old-fashioned courtesy which was full of charm. She had been thrown from a carriage the year before, and had never since been able to come downstairs or to mingle in the family life.

"They come to me instead," she told Katy. "There is no lack of pleasant company," she added; "everyone is very good to me. I have a reader for two hours a day, and I read to myself a little, and play Patience and Solitaire, and never lack entertainment."

There was something restful in the sight of such a lovely specimen of old age. Katy realised, as she looked at her, what a loss it had been to her own life that she had never known either of her grandparents. She sat and gazed at old Mrs. Redding with a mixture of regret and fascination. She longed to hold her hand, and kiss her, and play with her beautiful silvery hair, as Rose did. Rose was evidently the old lady's darling. They were on the most intimate terms; and Rose talked nonsense as freely as to a person of her own age. It was a delightful relation.

"Grandmamma has taken a fancy to you, I can see," she told

Katy, as they drove back to Longwood. " She always wants to know my friends ; and she has her own opinions about them, I can tell you."

" Do you really think she liked me ? " said Katy warmly. " I am so glad if she did, for I *loved* her. I never saw a really beautiful old person before."

" Oh, there's nobody like her ! " rejoined Rose. " I can't imagine what it would be not to have her." Her merry little face was quite sad and serious as she spoke. " I wish she were not so old," she added, with a sigh. " If we could only put her back twenty years ! Then, perhaps, she would live as long as I do."

The second day of Katy's visit was devoted to the luncheon-party of which Rose had written in her letter, and which was meant to be a reunion or " side chapter " of the S.S.U.C. Rose had asked every old Hillsover girl who was within reach. There was Mary Silver, of course, and Esther Dearborn, both of whom lived in Boston ; and by good luck Alice Gibbons happened to be making Esther a visit, and Ellen Gray came in from Waltham, where her father had recently been settled over a parish, so that altogether they made six of the original nine of the society.

The girls all seemed wonderfully unchanged to Katy, but they professed to find her very grown-up and dignified.

" I wonder if I am," she said. " Clover never told me so. But perhaps she has grown dignified too."

" Nonsense ! " cried Rose ; " Clover could no more be dignified than my baby could. Mary Silver, give me that child this moment ! I never saw such a greedy thing as you are ; you have kept her to yourself at least a quarter of an hour, and it isn't fair."

" Oh, I beg your pardon ! " said Mary, laughing and covering her mouth with her hand exactly in her old, shy, half-frightened way.

" We only need Mrs. Nipson to make our little party complete," went on Rose, " or dear Miss Jane ! What has become of Miss Jane, by the way ? Do any of you know ? "

" Oh, she is still teaching at Hillsover and waiting for her missionary ! He has never come back."

" What a shame ! " said Katy, though she could not help
laughing. " Miss Jane was really quite nice—no, not *nice*
exactly, but she had good things about her."

" Had she ? " remarked Rose satirically. " I never observed
them. It requires eyes like yours, real ' double million magnify-
ing-glasses of h'extra power,' to find them out. She was all
teeth and talons as far as I was concerned ; but I think she
really did have a softish spot in her old heart for you, Katy, and
it's the only good thing I ever knew about her."

" What has become of Lilly Page ? " asked Ellen.

" She's in Europe with her mother. I dare say you'll meet,
Katy, and what a pleasure that will be ! And have you heard
about Bella ? She's teaching school in the Indian Territory.
Just fancy that scrap teaching school ! "

It was a merry luncheon indeed, as little Rose seemed to
think, for she laughed and cooed incessantly. The girls were
enchanted with her, and voted her by acclamation an honorary
member of the S.S.U.C. Her health was drunk in Apollinaris
water with all the honours and Rose returned thanks in a droll
speech. The friends told each other their histories for the past
three years ; but it was curious how little, on the whole, most
of them had to tell. Though, perhaps, that was because they
did not tell all ; for Alice Gibbons confided to Katy in a whisper
that she strongly suspected Esther of being engaged and at the
same moment Ellen Gray was convulsing Rose by the intelligence that a theological student from Andover was " very
attentive " to Mary Silver.

" My dear, I don't believe it," Rose said ; " not even a
theological student would dare ! And if he did, I am quite sure
Mary would consider it most improper. You must be mistaken,
Ellen."

" No, I'm not mistaken ; for the theological student is my
second cousin. They are not engaged exactly, but she hasn't said
no ; so he hopes she will say yes."

" Oh, she'll never say no ; but then she will never say yes,
either ! He would better take silence as consent ! Well, I never
did think I should live to see Silvery Mary married. She's a
dear old thing, though, and as good as gold ; and I shall consider your second cousin a lucky man if he persuades her."

" I wonder where we shall all be when you return, Katy,"
said Esther Dearborn, as they parted. " A year is a long time ;
all sorts of things may happen in a year."

These words rang in Katy's ears as she fell asleep that night.
All sorts of things may happen in a year, she thought,
and they may not be all happy things, either. Almost she
wished that the journey to Europe had never been thought of !

Next morning she and Rose went early into town, for old
Mrs. Redding had made Katy promise to come to say good-bye.
They found her sitting by the fire as usual, though her windows
were open to admit the sun-warmed air. A little basket of
grapes stood on the table beside her, with a nosegay of tea-
roses on top. These were from Rose's mother, for Katy to take
on board the steamer ; and there was something else, a small
parcel twisted up in thin white paper.

" It is my good-bye gift," said the dear old lady. " Don't
open it now. Keep it till you are well out at sea, and get some
little thing with it as a keepsake from me."

Grateful and wondering, Katy put the little parcel in her
pocket. With kisses and good wishes she parted from these new-
made friends, and she and Rose drove to the steamer, stopping
for Mr. Browne by the way. They were a little late, so there
was not much time for farewells.

The bell rang, and the great steam-vessel slowly backed into
the stream. Then her head was turned to sea, and down the
bay she went, leaving Rose and her husband still waving their
handkerchiefs on the pier. Katy watched them to the last, and
when she could no longer distinguish them, felt that her final
link with home was broken.

It was not till she had settled her things in the little cabin
which was to be her home for the next ten days, that she found
time to examine the mysterious parcel.

Behold, it was a large, beautiful gold-piece twenty dollars !

" What a darling old lady ! " said Katy ; and she gave the
gold-piece a kiss. " How did she come to think of such a thing ?
I wonder if there is anything in Europe good enough to buy
with it ? "

CHAPTER IV

ON THE "SPARTACUS"

A FEW hours out a head-wind lay waiting in the offing, and the *Spartacus* began to pitch and toss in a manner which made all her unseasoned passengers glad to betake themselves to their berths. Mrs. Ashe and Amy were among the earliest victims of sea-sickness; and Katy, after helping them to settle in their state-rooms, found herself too dizzy and ill to sit up a moment longer, and thankfully resorted to her own.

As the night came on, the wind grew stronger and the motion worse. The *Spartacus* had the reputation of being a dreadful "roller," and seemed bound to justify it on this particular voyage. The night seemed endless, for she was too frightened to sleep except in broken snatches; and when day dawned, and she looked through the little round pane of glass in the port-hole, only grey sky and grey weltering waves and flying spray and rain met her view.

" Oh, dear, why do people ever go to sea, unless they must ? " she thought feebly to herself. She wanted to get up and see how Mrs. Ashe had lived through the night, but the attempt to move made her so miserably ill that she was glad to sink again on her pillows.

The stewardess looked in with offers of tea and toast, the very idea of which was simply dreadful, and pronounced the other lady " 'orribly ill, worse than you are, Miss," and the little girl " takin' on dreadful in the h'upper berth." Of this fact Katy soon had audible proof; for as her dizzy senses rallied a little, she could hear Amy in the opposite state-room crying and sobbing pitifully. She seemed to be angry as well as sick, for she was scolding her poor mother in the most vehement fashion.

" I hate being at sea," Katy heard her say. " I won't stay in this nasty old ship. Mamma! Mamma! Do you hear me? I won't stay in this ship ! It wasn't a bit kind of you to bring me to such a horrid place. It was very un-kind ; it was cru-el. I want to go back, Mamma. Tell the captain to take me back to the land. Mamma, why don't you speak to me ? Oh, I am so sick and so very un-happy ! Don't you wish you were dead ? I do ! "

And then came another storm of sobs, but never a sound from Mrs. Ashe, who, Katy suspected, was too ill to speak. She felt very sorry for poor little Amy, raging there in her high berth like some imprisoned creature, but she was powerless to help her. She could only resign herself to her own discomforts, and try to believe that somehow, sometime, this state of things must mend—either they should all get to land or all go to the bottom and be drowned, and at that moment she didn't care very much which it turned out to be.

The gale increased as the day wore on, and the vessel pitched dreadfully. Twice Katy was thrown out of her berth on the floor ; then the stewardess came and fixed a sort of movable side to the berth, which held her in, but made her feel like a child fastened into a railed crib. At intervals she could still hear Amy crying and scolding her mother, and conjectured that they were having a dreadful time of it in the other state-room. It was all like a bad dream. And they call this travelling for pleasure, thought poor Katy.

During the night the gale abated, the sea became smoother, and she dropped asleep. When she woke the sun was struggling through the clouds, and she felt better.

The stewardess opened the port-hole to freshen the air, and helped her to wash her face and smooth her tangled hair ; then she produced a little basin of gruel and a triangular piece of toast, and Katy found that her appetite was come again and she could eat.

She managed to struggle into her dressing-gown and slippers and across the entry to Mrs. Ashe's state-room. Amy had fallen asleep at last and must not be waked up, so their interview was conducted in whispers. Mrs. Ashe had by no means got to the tea-and-toast stage yet, and was feeling miserable enough.

" I have had the most dreadful time with Amy," she said. " All day yesterday, when she wasn't sick, she was raging at me from the upper berth, and I too ill to say a word in reply. I never knew her so naughty ! And it seemed very neglectful not to come to see after you, poor dear child ! But really I couldn't raise my head."

" Neither could I, and I felt just as guilty not to be taking care of you," said Katy. " Well, the worst is over with all of us, I hope. The vessel doesn't pitch half so much now, and the stewardess says we shall feel a great deal better as soon as we get on deck. She is coming presently to help me up ; and when Amy wakes, won't you let her be dressed, and I will take care of her while Mrs. Barrett attends to you ? "

" I don't think I can be dressed," sighed poor Mrs. Ashe. " I feel as if I should just lie here till we get to Liverpool."

" Oh no, h'indeed, mum—no, you won't," put in Mrs. Barrett, who at that moment appeared, gruel-cup in hand. " I don't never let my ladies lie in their berths a moment longer than there is need of. I h'always gets them on deck as soon as possible to get the h'air. It's the best medicine you can 'ave, ma'am, the fresh h'air ; h'indeed it h'is."

Stewardesses are all-powerful on board ship, and Mrs. Barrett was so persuasive as well as positive that it was not possible to resist her. She got Katy into her dress and wraps, and seated her on deck in a chair with a great rug wrapped about her feet. Then she dived down the companion-way again, and in the course of an hour appeared escorting a big, burly steward, who carried poor little pale Amy in his arms as easily as though she had been a kitten. Amy gave a scream of joy at the sight of Katy, and cuddled down in her lap under the warm rug with a sigh of relief and satisfaction.

" I thought I was never going to see you again," she said, with a little squeeze. " Oh, Miss Katy, it has been so horrid ! I never thought that going to Europe meant such dreadful things as this ! "

" This is only the beginning ; we shall get across the sea in a few days, and then we shall find out what going to Europe really means. But what made you behave so, Amy, and cry and scold poor mamma when she was sick ? I could hear you all the way across the entry."

" Could you ? Then, why didn't you come to me ? "

" I wanted to ; but I was sick too, so sick that I couldn't move. But why were you so naughty ?—you didn't tell me."

" I didn't mean to be naughty, but I couldn't help crying. You would have cried too, and so would Johnnie, if you had been cooped up in a dreadful old berth at the top of the wall that you couldn't get out of, and hadn't had anything to eat, and nobody to bring you any water when you wanted some. And mamma wouldn't answer when I called to her."

" She couldn't answer ; she was too ill," explained Katy. " Well, my pet, it *was* pretty hard for you. I hope we shan't have any more such days. The sea is a great deal smoother now."

A good many passengers had come up by this time ; and Robert, the deck steward, was going about, tray in hand, taking orders for lunch. Amy and Katy both felt suddenly ravenous ; and when Mrs. Ashe a while later was helped up the stairs, she was amazed to find them eating cold beef and roasted potatoes, with the finest appetites in the world. They had served out their apprenticeships, the kindly old captain told them, and were made free of the nautical guild from that time on. So it proved, for after these two bad days none of the party were sick again during the voyage.

Amy had a clamorous appetite for stories as well as for cold beef ; and to appease this craving, Katy started a sort of ocean serial, called " The History of Violet and Emma," which she meant to make last till they got to Liverpool, but which in reality lasted much longer. It might with equal propriety have been called " The Adventures of two little Girls who didn't have any Adventures," for nothing in particular happened to either Violet or Emma during the whole course of their long drawn-out history. Amy, however, found them perfectly enchanting, and was never weary of hearing how they went to school and came home again, how they got into scrapes and got out of them, how they made good resolutions and broke them, about their Christmas presents and birthday treats, and what they said and how they felt. The first instalment of this unexciting romance was given that first afternoon on deck ; and after that, Amy claimed a new chapter daily, and it was a chief ingredient of her pleasure during the voyage.

On the third morning Katy woke and dressed so early that she gained the deck before the sailors had finished their scrubbing and holy-stoning. She took refuge within the companionway, and sat down on the top step of the ladder, to wait till the deck was dry enough to venture upon it. There the Captain found her and drew near for a talk.

Captain Bryce was exactly the kind of sea-captain that is found in story-books, but not always in real life. He was stout, and grizzled, and brown, and kind. He had a bluff, weatherbeaten face, lit up with a pair of shrewd blue eyes which twinkled when he was pleased; and his manner, though it was full of the habit of command, was quiet and pleasant. He was a martinet on board his ship. Not a sailor under him would have dared dispute his orders for a moment; but he was very popular with them, notwithstanding; they liked him as much as they feared him, for they knew him to be their best friend if it came to sickness or trouble with any of them.

Katy and he grew quite intimate during their long morning talk. The Captain liked girls. He had one of his own, about Katy's age, and was fond of talking about her. Lucy was his mainstay at home, he told Katy. Her mother had been " weakly " now this long time back, and Bess and Nanny were but children yet, so Lucy had to take command and keep things ship-shape when he was away.

" She'll be on the look-out when the steamer comes in," said the Captain. " There's a signal we've arranged which means ' All's well,' and when we get up the river a little way I always look to see if it's flying. It's a bit of a towel hung from a particular window; and when I see it I say to myself, ' Thank God! another voyage safely done and no harm come of it.' It's a sad kind of work for a man to go off for a twenty-four days' cruise leaving a sick wife on shore behind him. If it wasn't that I have Lucy to look after things, I should have thrown up my command long ago."

" Indeed, I am glad you have Lucy; she must be a great comfort to you," said Katy, sympathetically; for the Captain's hearty voice trembled a little as he spoke. She made him tell her the colour of Lucy's hair and eyes, and exactly how tall she was, and what she had studied, and what sort of books she liked. She seemed such a very nice girl, and Katy thought she should like to know her.

Later in the morning, Katy, going down to her state-room for something, came across a pallid, exhausted-looking lady, who lay stretched on one of the long sofas in the cabin, with a baby in her arms and a little girl sitting at her feet, quite still, with a pair of small hands folded in her lap. The little girl did not seem to be more than four years old. She had two pig-tails of thick flaxen hair hanging over her shoulders, and at Katy's approach raised a pair of solemn blue eyes, which had so much appeal in them, that Katy stopped at once.

" Can I do anything for you ? " she asked. " I am afraid you have been very ill."

At the sound of her voice the lady on the sofa opened her eyes. She tried to speak, but to Katy's dismay began to cry instead ; and when the words came they were strangled with sobs.

" You are so kin-d to ask," she said. " If you would give my little girl something to eat ! She has had nothing since yesterday, and I have been so ill ; and nobody has c-ome near us ! "

" Oh ! " cried Katy, with horror, " nothing to eat since yesterday ! How did it happen ? "

" Everybody has been sick on our side of the ship," explained the poor lady, " and I suppose the stewardess thought, as I had a maid with me, that I needed her less than the others. But my maid has been sick too ; and oh, so selfish ! She wouldn't even take the baby into the berth with her ; and I have had all I could do to manage with him, when I couldn't lift up my head. Little Gretchen has had to go without anything ; and she has been so good and patient ! "

Katy lost no time, but ran for Mrs. Barrett, whose indignation knew no bounds when she heard how the helpless party had been neglected.

" It's a new person that stewardess h'is, ma'am," she explained, " and most h'inefficient ! I told the Captain when she came aboard that I didn't 'ave much opinion of her, and now he'll see how it h'is. I'm h'ashamed that such a thing should 'appen on the *Spartacus*, ma'am—I h'am, h'indeed. H'it never would 'ave been so h'under h'Eliza, ma'am—she's the one that went h'off and got herself married the trip before last, when this person came to take her place."

All the time that she talked Mrs. Barrett was busy in making Mrs. Ware—for that, it seemed, was the sick lady's name—more comfortable ; and Katy was feeding Gretchen out of a big bowl full of bread-and-milk which one of the stewards had brought. The little uncomplaining thing was evidently half-starved, but with the mouthfuls the pink began to steal back into her cheeks and lips, and the dark circles lessened under the blue eyes. By the time the bottom of the bowl was reached she could smile, but still she said not a word except a whispered *danke schön.* Her mother explained that she had been born in Germany, and always had till now been cared for by a German nurse, so that she knew the language better than English.

Gretchen was a great amusement to Katy and Amy during the rest of the voyage. They kept her on deck with them a great deal, and she was perfectly content with them and very good, though always solemn and quiet. Pleasant people turned up among the passengers, as always happens on an ocean steamship, and others not so pleasant, perhaps, who were rather curious and interesting to watch.

On the whole, there was no one on the *Spartacus* whom Katy liked so well as sedate little Gretchen except the dear old captain, with whom she was a prime favourite. He gave Mrs. Ashe and herself the seats next to him at table, looked after their comfort in every possible way, and each night at dinner sent Katy one of the apple-dumplings made specially for him by the cook, who had gone many voyages with the captain and knew his fancies. Katy did not care particularly for the dumpling, but she valued it as a mark of regard, and always ate it when she could.

Katy never forgot the thrill that went through her when, after so many days at sea, her eyes first caught sight of the dim line of the Irish coast. An exciting and interesting day followed as, after stopping at Queenstown to leave the mails, they sped north-eastwards between shores which grew more distinct and beautiful with every hour—on one side Ireland, on the other the bold mountain lines of the Welsh coast. It was late afternoon when they entered the Mersey, and dusk had fallen before the captain got out his glass to look for the white, fluttering speck in his own window which meant so much to him. Long he studied before he made quite sure that it was there. At last he shut the glass with a satisfied air.

"It's all right," he said to Katy, who stood near, almost as much interested as he. "Lucy never forgets, bless her! Well, there's another voyage over and done with, thank God, and my Mary is where she was. It's a load taken from my mind."

The moon had risen and was shining softly on the river as the crowded tender landed the passengers from the *Spartacus* at the Liverpool docks.

"We shall meet again in London or in Paris," said one to another, and cards and addresses were exchanged. Then, after a brief delay at the Customs they separated, each to his own particular destination.

"Four-wheeler or hansom, ma'am?" said a porter to Mrs. Ashe.

"Which, Katy?"

"Oh, let us have a hansom! I never saw one, and they look so nice in *Punch*."

So a hansom cab was called, the two ladies got in, Amy cuddled down between them, the folding doors were shut over their knees like a lap-robe, and away they drove up the solidly paved streets to the hotel where they were to pass the night. It was too late to see or do anything but enjoy the sense of being on firm land once more.

"How lovely it will be to sleep in a bed that doesn't tip or roll from side to side!" said Mrs. Ashe.

"Yes and one that is wide enough and long enough and soft enough to be comfortable!" replied Katy. "I feel as if I could sleep for a fortnight to make up for the bad nights at sea."

Everything seemed delightful to her—the space for undressing, the great tub of fresh water which stood beside the English-looking washstand with its ample basin and ewer, the chintz-curtained bed, the coolness, the silence—and she closed her eyes with the pleasant thought in her mind, "It is really England and we are really here!"

CHAPTER V

STORY-BOOK ENGLAND

" OH, is it raining ? " was Katy's first question next morning, when the maid came to call her. The pretty room, with its gaily flowered chintz, and china, and its brass bedstead, did not look half so bright as when lit with gas the night before ; and a dim grey light struggled in at the window, which in America would certainly have meant bad weather coming or already come.

" Oh no, h'indeed, ma'am, it's a very fine day—not bright, ma'am, but very dry," was the answer.

Katy couldn't imagine what the maid meant, when she peeped between the curtains and saw a thick dull mist lying over everything, and the pavement opposite her window shining with wet. Afterwards, when she understood better the peculiarities of the English climate, she too learned to call days not absolutely rainy " fine," and to be grateful for them ; but on that first morning her sensations were of bewildered surprise, almost vexation.

Mrs. Ashe and Amy were waiting in the coffee-room when she went in search of them.

" What shall we have for breakfast," asked Mrs. Ashe— " our first meal in England ? Katy, you order it."

" Let's have all the things we have read about in books and don't have at home," said Katy eagerly. But when she came to look over the bill of fare there didn't seem to be many such things. Soles and muffins she finally decided upon, and, as an afterthought, gooseberry-jam.

" Muffins sound so good in Dickens, you know," she explained to Mrs. Ashe ; " and I have never seen a sole."

The soles when they came proved to be nice little pan-fish, not unlike what in New England are called " scup." All the party took kindly to them ; but the muffins were a great disappointment, tough and tasteless, with a flavour about them as of scorched flannel.

48

"How queer and disagreeable they are!" said Katy. "I feel as if I were eating rounds cut from an old ironing-blanket and buttered! Dear me! What did Dickens mean by making such a fuss about them, I wonder? And I don't care for gooseberry jam, either; it isn't half as good as the jams we have at home. Books are very deceptive."

"I am afraid they are. We must make up our minds to find a great many things not quite so nice as they sound when we read about them," replied Mrs. Ashe.

Amy's doll, Mabel, was breakfasting with them, and was heard to remark at this juncture that she didn't like muffins either, and would a great deal rather have waffles; whereupon Amy reproved her, and explained that nobody in England knew what waffles were, they were such a stupid nation, and that Mabel must learn to eat whatever was given her and not find fault!

After this moral lesson it was found to be dangerously near train-time; and they all hurried to the railroad station, which, fortunately, was close by. There was rather a scramble and confusion for a few moments; for Katy, who had undertaken to buy the tickets, was puzzled by the unaccustomed coinage; and Mrs. Ashe, whose part was to see after the luggage, found herself perplexed and worried by the absence of checks, and by no means disposed to accept the porter's statement, that if she'd only bear in mind that the trunks were in the second van from the engine, and got out to see that they were safe once or twice during the journey, and call for them as soon as they reached London, she'd have no trouble—"please remember the porter, ma'am!" However all was happily settled at last; and without any serious inconveniences they found themselves established in a first-class carriage, presently running smoothly at full speed across the rich English Midlands towards London and the eastern coast.

Their destination in London was Batt's Hotel in Dover Street. The old gentleman on the *Spartacus,* who had "crossed" so many times, had furnished Mrs. Ashe with a number of addresses of hotels and lodging-houses, from among which Katy had chosen Batt's for the reason that it was mentioned in Miss Edgeworth's *Patronage.* "It was the place," she explained,

" where Godfrey Percy didn't stay when Lord Oldborough sent him the letter." It seemed an odd enough reason for going anywhere, that a person in a novel didn't stay there. But Mrs. Ashe knew nothing of London, and had no preference of her own ; so she was perfectly willing to give Katy hers, and Batt's was decided upon.

" It is just like a dream or a story," said Katy as they drove away from the London station in a four-wheeler. " It is really ourselves, and this is really London. Can you imagine it ? "

She looked out. Nothing met her eyes but dingy weather, muddy streets, long rows of ordinary brick or stone houses. It might very well have been New York or Boston on a foggy day, yet to her eyes all things had a subtle difference which made them unlike similar objects at home.

" Wimpole Street ! " she cried suddenly, as she caught sight of the name on the corner, " that is the street where Maria Crawford in *Mansfield Park*, you know, ' opened one of the best houses ' after she married Mr. Rushworth. Think of seeing Wimpole Street ! What fun ! " She looked eagerly out after the " best houses," but the whole street looked uninteresting and old-fashioned ; the best house to be seen was not of a kind, Katy thought, to reconcile an ambitious young woman to a dull husband. Katy had to remind herself that Miss Austen wrote her novels nearly a century ago, that London was a " growing " place, and that things were probably much changed since that day.

More " fun " awaited them when they arrived at Batt's, and exactly such a landlady sailed forth to welcome them as they had often met with in books—an old lady, smiling and rubicund, with a towering lace cap on her head, a flowered silk gown, a gold chain, and a pair of fat mittened hands demurely crossed over a black brocade apron. She alone would have been worth crossing the ocean to see, they all declared. Their telegram had been received, and rooms were ready, with a bright, smoky fire of soft coals ; the dinner-table was set, and a nice, formal, white-cravatted old waiter, who seemed to have stepped out of the same book with the landlady, was waiting to serve it. Everything was dingy and old-fashioned, but very clean and comfortable ; and Katy concluded that on the whole Godfrey

Percy would have done wisely to go to Batt's, and could have fared no better at the other hotel where he did stay.

The first of Katy's "London sights" came to her next morning before she was out of her bedroom : she heard a bell ring and a queer, squeaking little voice utter a speech of which she could not make out a single word. Then came a laugh and a shout, as if several boys were amused at something or other ; and altogether her curiosity was roused, so that she finished dressing as fast as she could, and ran to the drawing-room window, which commanded a view of the street. Quite a little crowd was collected under the window, and in their midst was a queer box raised high on poles, with little red curtains tied back on either side to form a miniature stage, on which puppets were moving and vociferating. Katy knew in a moment that she was seeing her first Punch and Judy !

The box and the crowd began to move away. Katy, in despair, ran to Wilkins, the old waiter, who was setting the breakfast-table.

" Oh, please stop that man ! " she said. " I want to see him."

" What man is it, miss ? " said Wilkins.

When he reached the window, and realised what Katy meant his sense of propriety seemed to receive a severe shock. He even ventured on remonstrance.

" H'I wouldn't, miss, h'if h'I was you. Them Punches are a low lot, miss ; they h'ought to be put down, really they h'ought. Gentlefolks, h'as a general thing, pays no h'attention to them."

But Katy didn't care what " gentlefolks " did or did not do, and insisted upon having Punch called back. So Wilkins was forced to swallow his remonstrances and his dignity, and go in pursuit of the objectionable object. Amy came rushing out, with her hair flying, and Mabel in her arms ; and she and Katy had a real treat of Punch and Judy, with all the well-known scenes, and perhaps a few new ones thrown in for their special behalf, for the showman seemed to be inspired by the rapturous enjoyment of his little audience of three at the first-floor window. Punch beat Judy and stole the baby, and Judy banged Punch in return, and the constable came in, and Punch outwitted him, and the hangman and the devil made their appearance duly ; and it was all perfectly satisfactory, and " just exactly what she hoped it would be, and it quite made up for the muffins," Katy declared.

Then, when Punch had gone away, the question arose as to what they should choose, out of the many delightful things in London, for their first morning.

Like ninety-nine Americans out of a hundred, they decided on Westminster Abbey ; and indeed there is nothing in England better worth seeing, or more impressive, in its dim, rich antiquity, to eyes fresh from the world which still calls itself " new." So to the Abbey they went, and lingered there till Mrs. Ashe declared herself to be absolutely dropping with fatigue.

" If you don't take me home and give me something to eat," she said, " I shall drop down on one of these pedestals and stay there and be exhibited for ever after as an ' h'effigy ' of somebody belonging to ancient English history."

So Katy tore herself away from Henry the Seventh and the Poets' corner, and tore Amy away from a quaint little tomb shaped like a cradle, with the marble image of a baby in it, which had greatly taken her fancy. She could only be consoled by the promise that she should soon come again and stay as long as she liked.

She reminded Katy of this promise the very next morning.

" Mamma has waked up with rather a bad headache, and she thinks she will lie still and not come to breakfast," she reported. " And she sends her love, and says will you please have a cab and go where you like ; and if I won't be a trouble, she would be glad if you would take me with you. And I won't be a trouble, Miss Katy, and I know where I wish you would go."

" Where is that ? "

" To see that cunning little baby again that we saw yesterday. I want to show her to Mabel—she didn't go with us, you know, and I don't like to have her mind not improved ; and, darling Miss Katy, mayn't I buy some flowers and put them on the baby ? She's so dusty and so old that I don't believe anybody has put any flowers for her for ever so long."

Katy found this idea rather pretty, and willingly stopped at Covent Garden, where they bought a bunch of late roses for eighteen pence, which entirely satisfied Amy. With them in her hand, and Mabel in her arms, she led the way through the dim aisles of the Abbey, through gates and doors, and up and down steps; the guide following, but not at all needed, for Amy seemed to have a perfectly clear recollection of every turn and winding. When the chapel was reached, she laid the roses on the tomb with gentle fingers, and a pitiful, reverent look in her grey eyes. Then she lifted Mabel up to kiss the odd little baby effigy above the marble quilt; whereupon the guide seemed altogether surprised out of his composure, and remarked to Katy:

"Little miss is an h'American, as is plain to see; no h'English child would be likely to think of doing such a thing."

"Do not English children take any interest in the tombs of the Abbey?" asked Katy.

"Oh, yes, m'm—h'interest; but they don't take no special notice of one tomb above h'another."

Katy could scarcely keep from laughing, especially as she heard Amy, who had been listening to the conversation, give an audible sniff, and inform Mabel that she was glad *she* was not an English child who didn't notice things, and liked grown-up graves as much as she did dear little cunning ones like this!

Later in the day, when Mrs. Ashe was better, they all drove together to the quaint old keep which has been the scene of so many tragedies, and is known as the Tower of London. Here they were shown various rooms and chapels and prisons; and among the rest the apartments where Queen Elizabeth, when a friendless young princess, was shut up for many months by her sister Queen Mary.

"If this is English History, I never mean to learn any more of it, and neither shall Mabel," she declared.

But it is not possible for Amy or anyone else not to learn a great deal of history simply by going about London. So many places are associated with people or events, and seeing the places makes one care so much more for the people or the events that one insensibly questions and wonders. Katy, who had "browsed" all through her childhood in a good old-fashioned library, had her memory stuffed with all manner of little scraps of information and literary allusions, which now came into use. It was like owning the disjointed bits of a puzzle, and suddenly discovering that properly put together they make a pattern. Mrs. Ashe, who had never been much of a reader, considered her young friend a prodigy of intelligence ; but Katy herself realised how inadequate and inexact her knowledge was, and how many bits were missing from the pattern of her puzzle. She wished with all her heart, as everyone wishes under such circumstances, that she had studied harder and more wisely while the chance was in her power.

October is not a favourable month in which to see England. Water, water is everywhere ; you breathe it ; you absorb it ; it wets your clothes and it dampens your spirits. Mrs. Ashe's friends advised her not to think of Scotland at that time of the year. One by one their little intended excursions were given up. A single day and night in Oxford and Stratford-on-Avon ; a short visit to the Isle of Wight, where, in a country-place which seemed provokingly pretty as far as they could see it for the rain, lived that friend of Mrs. Ashe who had married an Englishman and in so doing had, as Katy privately thought, " renounced the sun "; a peep at Stonehenge from under the shelter of an umbrella, and an hour or two in Salisbury Cathedral—was all that they accomplished, except a brief halt at Winchester, that Katy might have the privilege of seeing the grave of her beloved Miss Austen. Katy had come abroad with a terribly long list of graves to visit, Mrs. Ashe declared. They laid a few rain-washed flowers upon the tomb, and listened with edification to the verger, who inquired :

" Whatever was it, ma'am, that lady did which brings so many h'Americans to h'ask about her ? Our h'English people don't seem to take the same h'interest."

" She wrote such delightful stories," explained Katy ; but the old verger shook his head.

" I think h'it must be some other party, miss, you've confused with this here. It stands to reason, miss, that we'd have heard of 'em h'over 'ere in England sooner than you would h'over there in h'America, if the books 'ad been h'anything so h'extraordinary."

The night after their return to London, they were dining for the second time with the cousins of whom Mrs. Ashe had spoken to Dr. Carr ; and as it happened Katy sat next to a quaint elderly American, who had lived for twenty years in London

and knew it much better than most Londoners do. This gentleman, Mr. Allen Beach, had a hobby for antiquities, old books
especially, and passed half his time at the British Museum, and
the other half in sale-rooms and the old shops in Wardour
Street.

Katy was lamenting over the bad weather which stood in the
way of their plans.

" It is so vexatious ! " she said. " Mrs. Ashe meant to go to
York and Lincoln and all the cathedral towns and to Scotland ;
and we have had to give it all up because of the rains. We shall
go away, having seen hardly anything."

" You can see London."

" We have—that is, we have seen the things that everybody
sees."

" But there are so many things that people in general do not
see. How much longer are you to stay, Miss Carr ? "

" A week, I believe."

" Why don't you make out a list of old buildings which are
connected with famous people in history, and visit them in
turn ? I did that the second year after I came. I gave up three
months to it, and it was most interesting. I unearthed all
manner of curious stories and traditions."

" Oh," cried Katy, struck with a sudden bright thought,
" why mightn't I put into the list some of the places I know
about in books—novels as well as history—and the places where
the people who wrote the books lived ? "

" You might do that, and it wouldn't be a bad idea, either,"
said Mr. Beach, pleased with her enthusiasm. " I will get a
pencil after dinner, and help you with your list if you will
allow me."

Mr. Beach was better than his word. He not only suggested
places and traced a plan of sight-seeing, but on two different
mornings he went with them himself.

With such a lot to see and to do, the last week sped all too
swiftly, and the last day came before they were at all ready to
leave what Katy called " Story-book England." Mrs. Ashe had
decided to cross by Newhaven and Dieppe, because someone
had told her of the beautiful old town of Rouen, and it seemed
easy and convenient to take it on the way to Paris. Just landed

from the long voyage across the Atlantic, the little passage of the Channel seemed nothing to our travellers, and they made ready for their night on the Dieppe steamer with the philosophy which is born of ignorance. They were speedily undeceived!

The English Channel has a character of its own, which distinguishes it from other seas and straits. It seems made fractious and difficult by nature, and set as on purpose to be a barrier between two nations who are too unlike to understand each other easily, and are the safer neighbours for this wholesome difficulty of communication between them. The "chop" was worse than usual on the night when our travellers crossed; the steamer had to fight her way inch by inch. And oh, such a little steamer! And oh, such a long night!

CHAPTER VI

ACROSS THE CHANNEL

DAWN had given place to day, and day was well advanced towards noon, before the stout little steamer gained her port. It was hours after the usual time of arrival; the train for Paris must long since have started, and Katy felt dejected and forlorn as, making her way out of the terrible ladies'-cabin, she crept on deck for her first glimpse of France.

The sun was struggling through the fog with a watery smile, and his faint beams shone on a confusion of stone piers, higher than the vessel's deck, intersected with canal-like waterways, through whose intricate windings the steamer was slowly threading her course to the landing-place. Looking up, Katy could see crowds of people assembled to watch the boat come in—workmen, peasants, women, children, soldiers, custom-house officers, moving to and fro—and all this crowd were talking at once and all were talking French.

" Oh dear, what is the word for trunk-key ? " she asked herself. " They will all begin to ask questions, and I shall not have a word to say; and Mrs. Ashe will be even worse off, I know."

She saw the red-trousered custom-house officers pounce upon the passengers as they landed one by one, and she felt her heart sink within her.

But after all, when the time came, it did not prove so very bad. Katy's pleasant looks and courteous manner stood her in good stead. She did not trust herself to say much ; but the officials seemed to understand without saying. They bowed and gestured, whisked the keys in and out, and in a surprisingly short time all was pronounced right, the baggage had " passed," and it and its owners were free to proceed to the railway station, which fortunately was close at hand.

Inquiry revealed the fact that no train for Paris left till four in the afternoon.

" I am rather glad," declared poor Mrs. Ashe, " for I feel too used up to move. I will lie here on this sofa ; and, Katy dear, please see if there is an eating-place, and get some breakfast for yourself and Amy, and send me a cup of tea."

" I don't like to leave you alone," Katy was beginning ; but at that moment a nice old woman, who seemed to be in charge of the waiting-room, appeared, and with a flood of French which none of them could follow, but which was evidently sympathetic in its nature, flew at Mrs. Ashe and began to make her comfortable. From a cupboard in the wall she produced a pillow, from another cupboard a blanket ; in a trice she had one under Mrs. Ashe's head and the other wrapped round her feet.

" Pauvre madame," she said. " Si pâle ! si souffrante ! Il faut avoir quelque chose à boire et à manger tout de suite." She trotted across the room and into the restaurant which opened out of it, while Mrs. Ashe smiled at Katy and said, " You see you can leave me quite safely ; I am to be taken care of." And Katy and Amy passed through the same door into the buffet, and sat down at a little table.

Fortified with a satisfactory breakfast, Katy felt equal to a walk ; and after they had made sure that Mrs. Ashe had all she needed, she and Amy (and Mabel) set off by themselves to see the sights of Dieppe. I don't know that travellers generally have considered Dieppe an interesting place, but Katy found it so. There was a really old church and some quaint buildings of the style of two centuries back, and even the more modern streets had a novel look to her unaccustomed eyes. At first they only ventured a timid turn or two, marking each corner, and going back now and then to reassure themselves by a look at the station ; but after a while, growing bolder, Katy ventured to ask a question or two in French, and was surprised and charmed to find herself understood. After that she grew adventurous, and, no longer fearful of being lost, led Amy straight down a long street lined with shops, almost all of which were for the sale of articles in ivory.

Ivory wares are one of the chief industries of Dieppe. There were cases full, windows full, counters full, of the most exquisite combs and brushes, some with elaborate monograms in silver and colours, others plain ; there were boxes and caskets of every size and shape, ornaments, fans, parasol handles, looking-glasses, frames for pictures large and small, napkin-rings.

Katy was particularly smitten with a paper-knife in the form of an angel with long, slender wings raised over its head and meeting to form a point. Its price was twenty francs, and she was strongly tempted to buy it for Clover or Rose Red. But she said to herself sensibly : " This is the first shop I have been into and the first thing I have really wanted to buy, and very likely as we go on I shall see things I like better and want more, so it would be foolish to do it. No, I won't." And she resolutely turned her back on the ivory angel, and walked away.

The next turn brought them to a gay-looking little market-place, where old women in white caps were sitting on the ground beside baskets and panniers full of apples, pears, and various queer and curly vegetables, none of which Katy recognised ; fish of all shapes and colours were flapping in shallow tubs of sea-water ; there were piles of stockings, muffettees, and comforters in vivid blue and red worsted, and coarse pottery glazed in bright patterns. The faces of the women were brown and wrinkled ; there were no pretty ones among them, but their black eyes were full of life and quickness, and their fingers clicked with knitting-needles, as their tongues flew equally fast in the chatter and the chaffer, which went on without stop or stay, though customers did not seem to be many and sales were few.

Returning to the station they found that Mrs. Ashe had been asleep during their absence, and seemed so much better that it was with greatly amended spirits that they took their places in the late afternoon train which was to set them down at Rouen. Katy said they were like the Wise Men of the East, " following a star," in their choice of a hotel ; for, having no better advice, they had decided upon one of those thus distinguished in Baedeker's Guide-book.

The star did not betray their confidence ; for the Hôtel de la Cloche, to which it led them, proved to be quaint and old, and very pleasant of aspect. The lofty chambers with their dimly frescoed ceilings, and beds curtained with faded patch, might to all appearances have been furnished about the time when " Columbus crossed the ocean blue "; but everything was clean, and had an air of old-time respectability. The dining-room, which was evidently of more modern build, opened into a square courtyard, where oleanders and lemon trees in boxes stood round the basin of a little fountain, whose tinkle and splash blended agreeably with the rattle of the knives and forks. In one corner of the room was a raised and railed platform, where, behind a desk, sat the mistress of the house, busy with her account-books, but keeping an eye the while on all that went forward.

The next day Mrs. Ashe, Katy and Amy toured the old city, rich in carvings and sculptures and traditions, and saw the Cathedral, the church of St. Ouen, the Palace of Justice, and the " Place of the Maid," where poor Jeanne d'Arc was burned and her ashes scattered to the winds.

Paris looked very modern after the peculiar quaint richness and air of the Middle Ages which distinguished Rouen. Rooms had been engaged for Mrs. Ashe's party in a *pension* near the Arc de l'Étoile, and there they drove immediately on arriving. The rooms were not in the *pension* itself, but in a house close by —a sitting-room with six mirrors, three clocks, and a pinched little grate about a foot wide, a dining-room just large enough for a table and four chairs, and two bedrooms. A maid called Amandine had been detailed to take charge of these rooms and serve their meals.

Dampness, as Katy afterwards wrote to Clover, was the first

impression they received of " gay Paris." The tiny fire in the tiny grate had only just be lighted, and the walls and the sheets and even the blankets felt chilly and moist to the touch. They spent their first evening in hanging the bed-clothes round the grate and piling on fuel; they even set the mattresses up on edge to warm and dry! It was not very enlivening, it must be confessed. Amy had taken a cold, Mrs. Ashe looked worried, and Katy thought of Burnet and the safety and comfort of home with a throb of longing.

The days that ensued were not brilliant enough to remove this impression. The November fogs seemed to have followed them across the Channel, and Paris remained enveloped in a wet blanket which dimmed and hid its usually brilliant features. Going about in cabs with the windows drawn up, and now and then making a rush through the drip into shops, was not exactly delightful, but it seemed pretty much all that they could do. It was worse for Amy, whose cold kept her indoors and denied her even the relaxation of the cab. Mrs. Ashe had engaged a well-recommended elderly English maid to come every morning and take care of Amy while they were out; and with this respectable functionary, whose ideas were of a rigidly British type, and who did not speak a word of any language but her own, poor Amy was compelled to spend most of her time.

Katy looked at Amy's pale little face and eager eyes with a real heartache. Her rapture when, at the end of the long dull afternoons, her mother returned to her was touching. Paris was very *triste* to poor Amy, with all her happy facility for amusing herself; and Katy felt that the sooner they got away from it the better it would be. So, in spite of the delight which her brief glimpses at the Louvre gave her, and the fun it was to go about with Mrs. Ashe and see her buy pretty things, and the real satisfaction she took in the one perfectly made walking-suit to which she had treated herself, she was glad when the final day came, when the belated dressmakers and artistes in jackets and wraps had sent home their last wares, and the trunks were packed. It had been rather the fault of circumstances than of Paris; but Katy had not learned to love the beautiful capital as most Americans do, and did not feel at all as if she wanted that her "reward of virtue" should be to go there when she died!

There must be more interesting places for live people, and ghosts too, to be found on the map of Europe, she was sure.

Next morning, as they drove slowly down the Champs Élysées, and looked back for a last glimpse of the famous Arch, a bright object met their eyes, moving vaguely against the mist. It was the gay red wagon of the Bon Marché, carrying bundles home to the dwellers of some up-town street.

Katy burst out laughing. " It is an emblem of Paris," she said—" of our Paris, I mean. It has been all Bon Marché and fog ! "

" Miss Katy," interrupted Amy, " *do* you like Europe ? For my part, I was never so disgusted with any place in my life ! "

" Poor little bird, her views of ' Europe ' are rather dark just now, and no wonder," said her mother. " Never mind, darling, you shall have something pleasanter by and by if I can find it for you."

" Burnet is a great deal pleasanter than Paris," pronounced Amy, decidedly. " It doesn't always keep raining there, and I can take walks, and I understand everything that people say."

All that day they sped southwards, and with every hour came a change in the aspect of their surroundings.

And when the long night ended and day roused them from broken slumbers, behold, the world was made over ! Autumn had vanished, and the summer, which they thought fled for good, had taken its place. Green woods waved about them, fresh leaves were blowing in the wind, roses and hollyhocks beckoned from white-walled gardens ; and before they had done with exclaiming and rejoicing, the Mediterranean shot into view, intensely blue, with white fringes of foam, white sails blowing across, white gulls flying above it, and over all a sky of the same exquisite blue, whose clouds were white as the drifting sails on the water below, and they were at Marseilles.

It was like a glimpse of Paradise to eyes fresh from autumnal greys and glooms, as they sped along the lovely coast, every curve and turn showing new combinations of sea and shore, olive-crowned cliff and shining mountain-peak. With every mile the blue became bluer, the wind softer, the feathery verdure more dense and summer-like. Hyeres and Cannes and Antibes were passed, and then, as they rounded a long point, came the view of a sunshine city lying on a sunlit shore; the train slackened its speed, and they knew that their journey's end was come and they were in Nice.

The place seemed to laugh with gaiety as they drove down the Promenade des Anglais and past the English garden, where the band was playing beneath the acacias and palm trees. On one side was a line of bright-windowed hotels and *pensions*, with balconies and striped awnings; on the other, the long reach of yellow sand-beach, where ladies were grouped on shawls and rugs, and children ran up and down in the sun, while beyond stretched the waveless sea. The December sun felt as warm as on a late June day at home, and had the same caressing touch. The pavements were thronged with groups of leisurely-looking people, all wearing an unmistakable holiday aspect; pretty girls in correct Parisian costumes walked demurely beside their mothers, with cavaliers in attendance; and among these young men appeared now and again the well-known uniform of the United States Navy.

" I wonder," said Mrs. Ashe, struck by a sudden thought, " if by any chance our squadron is here." She asked the question the moment they entered the hotel; and the porter, who prided himself on understanding " zose Eenglesh," replied:

" Mai oui, madame, za Americaine fleet it is here; zat is, not here, but at Villefranche, just a leetle four mile away—it is ze same zing exactly."

" Katy, do you hear that ? " cried Mrs. Ashe. " The frigates *are* here, and the *Natchitoches* among them of course; and we shall have Ned to go about with us everywhere. It is a real piece of good luck for us. Ladies are at such a loss in a place like this, with nobody to escort them. I am perfectly delighted."

" So am I," said Katy. " I never saw a frigate, and I always wanted to see one. Do you suppose they will let us go on board them ? "

" Why, of course they will." Then to the porter : " Give me a sheet of paper and an envelope, please—I must let Ned know that I am here at once."

Mrs. Ashe wrote her note and despatched it before they went

upstairs to take off their bonnets. She seemed to have a half-hope that some bird of the air might carry the news of her arrival to her brother, for she kept running to the window as if in expectation of seeing him. She was too restless to lie down or sleep, and after she and Katy had lunched, proposed that they should go out on the beach for a while.

" Perhaps we may come across Ned," she remarked.

They did not come across Ned, but there was no lack of other delightful objects to engage their attention. The sands were smooth and hard as a floor. Soft pink lights were beginning to tinge the western sky. To the north shone the peaks of the maritime Alps, and the same rosy glow caught them here and there, and warmed their greys and whites into colour.

" I wonder what that can be ! " said Katy, indicating the rocky point which bounded the beach to the east, where stood a picturesque building of stone, with massive towers and steep pitches of roof. " It looks half like a house and half like a castle, but it is quite fascinating, I think. Do you suppose that people live there ? "

" We might ask," suggested Mrs. Ashe.

Just then they came to a shallow river spanned by a bridge, beside whose pebbly bed stood a number of women who seemed to be washing clothes by the simple and primitive process of laying them in the water on top of the stones, and pounding them with a flat wooden paddle till they were white. Katy privately thought that the clothes stood a poor chance of lasting through these cleansing operations ; but she did not say so, and made the inquiry which Mrs. Ashe had suggested, in her best French.

" *Celle-là* ? " answered the old woman whom she had addressed. " *Mais c'est la Pension Suisse.*"

" A *pension* ! Why, that means a boarding-house ! " cried Katy. " What fun it must be to board there ! "

" Well, why shouldn't we board there ? " said her friend. " You know we meant to look for rooms as soon as we were rested and had found out a little about the place. Let us walk on and see what the Pension Suisse is like. If the inside is as pleasant as the outside, we could not do better, I should think."

" Oh, I do hope all the rooms are not already taken ! " said

Katy, who had fallen in love at first sight with the Pension Suisse. She felt quite oppressed with anxiety as they rang the bell.

The Pension Suisse proved to be quite as charming inside as out. The thick stone walls made deep sills and embrasures for the casement windows, which were furnished with red cushions to serve as seats and lounging-places. Every window seemed to command a view, for those which did not look towards the sea looked towards the mountains. The house was by no means full either. Several sets of rooms were to be had ; and Katy felt as if she had walked straight into the pages of a romance when Mrs. Ashe engaged for a month a delightful suite of three, a sitting-room and two sleeping-chambers, in a round tower, with a balcony overhanging the water, and a side window, from which a flight of steps led down into a little walled garden, nestled in among the masonry, where tall laurustinus and lemon-trees grew, and orange and brown wall-flowers made the air sweet. Her contentment knew no bounds.

" I am so glad that I came ! " she told Mrs. Ashe. " I never confessed it to you before, but sometimes—when we were sick at sea, you know, and when it would rain all the time, and after Amy caught that cold in Paris—I have almost wished, just for a minute or two at a time, that we hadn't. But now I wouldn't not have come for the world ! This is perfectly delicious. I am glad, glad, glad we are here, and we are going to have a lovely time, I know."

They were passing out of the rooms into the hall as she said these words, and two ladies who were walking up a cross passage turned their heads at the sound of her voice. To her great surprise Katy recognised Mrs. Page and Lilly.

" Why, Cousin Olivia, is it you ? " she cried, springing forward with the cordiality one naturally feels in seeing a familiar face in a foreign land.

Mrs. Page seemed puzzled rather than cordial. She put up her eye-glass and did not seem to quite make out who Katy was.

" It is Katy Carr, Mamma," explained Lilly. " Well, Katy, this *is* a surprise ! Who would have thought of meeting you in Nice ? "

There was a decided absence of rapture in Lilly's manner. She was prettier than ever, as Katy saw in a moment, and beautifully dressed in soft brown velvet, which exactly suited her complexion and her pale-coloured wavy hair.

" Katy Carr ! Why, so it is !" admitted Mrs. Page. " It is a surprise indeed. We had no idea that you were abroad. What has brought you so far from Tunket—Burnet, I mean ? Who are you with ? "

" With my friend Mrs. Ashe," explained Katy, rather chilled by this cool reception. " Let me introduce you. Mrs. Ashe, these are my cousins, Mrs. Page and Miss Page. Amy—why, where is Amy ? "

Amy had walked back to the door of the garden staircase, and was standing there looking down upon the flowers.

Cousin Olivia bowed rather distantly. Her quick eye took in the details of Mrs. Ashe's travelling-dress and Katy's dark-blue ulster.

" Some countrified friend from that dreadful Western town where they live," she said to herself. " How foolish of Philip Carr to try to send his girls to Europe ! He can't afford it, I know." Her voice was rather rigid as she inquired :

" And what brings you here—to this house, I mean ? "

" Oh, we are coming to-morrow to stay ! We have taken rooms for a month," explained Katy. " What a delicious-looking old place it is ! "

" Have you ? " said Lilly, in a voice which did not express any particular pleasure. " Why, we are staying here too."

CHAPTER VII

THE PENSION SUISSE

" WHAT do you suppose can have brought Katy Carr to Europe ? " inquired Lilly, as she stood in the window watching the three figures walk slowly down the sands. " She is the last person I expected to turn up here. I supposed she was stuck in that horrid place—what is the name of it ?—where they live, for the rest of her life."

" I confess I am surprised at meeting her myself," rejoined Mrs. Page. " I had no idea that her father could afford so expensive a journey."

" And who is this woman that she has got along with her ? "

" I have no idea, I'm sure. Some Western friend, I suppose."

" Dear me ! I wish they were going to some other house than this," said Lilly discontentedly. " If they were at the Rivoir, for instance, or one of those places at the far end of the beach, we shouldn't need to see anything of them, or even know that they were in town ! It's a real nuisance to have people spring upon you this way, people you don't want to meet ; and when they happen to be relations it is all the worse. Katy will be hanging on us all the time, I'm afraid."

" Oh, my dear, there is no fear of that ! A little repression on our part will prevent her from being any trouble, I'm quite certain. But we *must* treat her politely, you know, Lilly, her father is my cousin."

" That's the saddest part of it ! Well, there's one thing, I shall *not* take her with me every time we go to the frigates," said Lilly decisively. " I am not going to inflict a country cousin on Lieutenant Worthington, and spoil all my own fun beside. So I give you fair warning, Mamma, and you must manage it some-how "

" Certainly, dear, I will. It would be a great pity to have your visit to Nice spoiled in any way, with the squadron here, too, and that pleasant Mr. Worthington so very attentive."

Unconscious of these plans for her suppression, Katy walked back to the hotel in a mood of pensive pleasure. Europe at last promised to be as delightful as it had seemed when she only knew it from maps and books, and Nice so far appeared to her the most charming place in the world.

Somebody was waiting for them at the Hôtel des Anglais— a tall, bronzed, good-looking somebody in uniform, with pleasant brown eyes beaming from beneath a gold-banded cap ; at the sight of whom Amy rushed forward with her long locks flying, and Mrs. Ashe uttered an exclamation of pleasure. It was Ned Worthington, Mrs. Ashe's only brother, whom she had not met for two years and a half.

" You got my note then ? " she said, after the first eager greetings were over and she had introduced him to Katy.

" Note ? No. Did you write me a note ? "

" Yes ; to Villefranche."

" To the ship ? I shan't get that till to-morrow. No ; finding out that you were here is just a bit of good fortune. I came over to call on some friends who are staying down the beach a little way, and, dropping in to look over the list of arrivals, as I generally do, I saw your names ; and the porter not being able to say which way you had gone, I waited for you to come in."

" We have been looking at such a delightful old place, the Pension Suisse, and have taken rooms."

" The Pension Suisse, eh ? Why, that was where I was going to call. I know some people who are staying there. It seems a pleasant house ; I'm glad you are going there, Polly. It's first-rate luck that the ships happen to be here just now. I can see you every day."

" But, Ned, surely you are not leaving me so soon ? Surely you will stay and dine with us ? " urged his sister, as he took up his cap.

" I wish I could, but I can't to-night, Polly. You see I had engaged to take some ladies out to drive, and they will expect me. I had no idea that you would be here, or I should have kept myself free," apologetically. " To-morrow I will come over early, and be at your service for whatever you like to do."

" That's right, dear boy. We shall expect you." Then the moment he was gone : " Now, Katy, isn't he nice ? "

" Very nice, I should think," said Katy, who had watched the brief interview with interest. " I like his face so much, and how fond he is of you ! "

" Dear fellow ! So he is. I am seven years older than he, but we have always been intimate. Brothers and sisters are not always intimate, you know—or perhaps you don't know, for all of yours are."

" Yes, indeed," said Katy, with a happy smile. " There is

nobody like Clover and Elsie, except perhaps Johnnie and Dorry and Phil," she added, with a laugh.

The remove to the Pension Suisse was made early the next morning. Mrs. Page and Lilly did not appear to welcome them. Katy rather rejoiced in their absence, for she wanted the chance to get into order without interruptions. There was something comfortable in the thought that they were to stay a whole month in these new quarters ; for so long a time it seemed worth while to make them pretty and homelike. So, while Mrs. Ashe unpacked her own belongings and Amy's, Katy, who had a natural turn for arranging rooms, took possession of the little parlour, pulled the furniture into new positions, laid out portfolios and work-cases and their few books, pinned various photographs which they had bought in Oxford and London on the walls, and tied back the curtains to admit the sunshine. Then she paid a visit to the little garden, and came back with a long branch of laurustinus, which she trained across the mantelpiece and a bunch of wallflowers for their one little vase. The maid, by her orders, laid a fire of wood and pine cones ready for lighting ; and when all was done she called Mrs. Ashe to pronounce upon the effect.

" It is lovely," she said, sinking into a great velvet armchair which Katy had drawn close to the seaward window. " I haven't seen anything so pleasant since we left home. You are a witch, Katy, and the comfort of my life. I am so glad I brought you ! Now, pray go and unpack your own things, and make yourself look nice for the second breakfast. We have been a shabby set enough since we arrived. I saw those cousins of yours looking askance at our old travelling-dresses yesterday. Let us try to make a more respectable impression to-day."

So they went down to breakfast, Mrs. Ashe in one of her new Paris gowns, Katy in a pretty dress of olive serge, and Amy all smiles and ruffled pinafore, walking hand in hand with her Uncle Ned, who had just arrived, and whose great ally she was ; and Mrs. Page and Lilly, who were already seated at table, had much ado to conceal their somewhat unflattering surprise at the conjunction. For one moment Lilly's eyes opened into a wild stare of incredulous astonishment ; then she remembered herself, nodded as pleasantly as she could to Mrs. Ashe and

Katy, and favoured Lieutenant Worthington with a pretty blushing smile as he went by, while she murmured :

" Mamma, do you see that ? What does it mean ? "

" Why, Ned, do you know those people ? " asked Mrs. Ashe at the same moment.

" Do *you* know them ? "

" Yes, we met yesterday. They are connections of my friend Miss Carr."

" Really ? There is not the least family likeness between them." And Mr. Worthington's eyes travelled deliberately from Lilly's delicate golden prettiness to Katy, who, truth to say, did not shine by the contrast.

She has a nice, sensible sort of face, he thought, and she looks like a lady, but for beauty there is no comparison between the two. Then he turned to listen to his sister as she replied :

" No, indeed, not the least ; no two girls could be less like." Mrs. Ashe had made the same comparison, but with quite a different result. Katy's face had grown dear to her, and she had not taken the smallest fancy to Lilly Page.

Her relationship to the young naval officer, however, made a wonderful difference in the attitude of Mrs. Page and Lilly towards the party. Katy became a person to be cultivated rather than repressed, and thence-forward there was no lack of cordiality on their part.

" I want to come in and have a good talk," said Lilly, slipping her arm through Katy's as they left the dining-room. " Mayn't I come now while mamma is calling on Mrs. Ashe ? " This arrangement brought her to the side of Lieutenant Worthington, and she walked between him and Katy down the hall and into the little drawing-room.

" Oh, how perfectly charming ! You have been fixing up ever since you came, haven't you ? It looks like home. I wish we had a *salon*, but mamma thought it wasn't worth while, as we were only to be here such a little time. What a delicious balcony over the water, too ! May I go out on it ? Oh, Mr. Worthington, do see this ! "

She pushed upon the half-closed window and stepped out as she spoke. Mr. Worthington, after hesitating a moment, followed. Katy paused uncertain. There was hardly room for three on the balcony, yet she did not quite like to leave them. But Lilly had turned her back, and was talking in a low tone ; it was nothing more in reality than the lightest chit-chat, but it had the air of being somewhat confidential ; so Katy, after waiting a little while, retreated to the sofa and took up her work, joining now and then in the conversation which Mrs. Ashe was keeping up with Cousin Olivia. She did not mind Lilly's ill breeding, nor was she surprised at it. Mrs. Ashe was less tolerant.

" Isn't it rather damp out there, Ned ? " she called to her brother ; " you had better throw my shawl round Miss Page's shoulders."

" Oh, it isn't a bit damp ! " said Lilly, recalled to herself by this broad hint. " Thank you so much for thinking of it, Mrs. Ashe, but I am just coming in." She seated herself beside Katy, and began to question her rather languidly.

" When did you leave home, and how were they all when you came away ? "

" All well, thank you. We sailed from Boston on the 14th of October, and before that I spent two days with Rose Red—you remember her ? She is married now, and has the dearest little home and such a darling baby ! "

" Yes, I heard of her marriage. It didn't seem much of a match for Mr. Redding's daughter to make, did it ? I never supposed she would be satisfied with anything less than a member of Congress or a Secretary of Legation."

" Rose isn't particularly ambitious, I think, and she seems perfectly happy," replied Katy flushing.

" Oh, you needn't fire up in her defence ! You and Clover always did adore Rose Red, I know, but I never could see what there was about her that was so wonderfully fascinating. She never had the least style, and she was always just as rude to me as she could be."

" You were not intimate at school, but I am sure Rose was never rude," said Katy with spirit.

" Well, we won't fight about her at this late day. Tell me where you have been, and where you are going, and how long you are to stay in Europe."

Katy, glad to change the subject, complied, and the conversation diverged into comparisons of plans and experiences. Lilly had been in Europe nearly a year, and had seen " almost everything," as she phrased it. She and her mother had spent the previous winter in Italy, had taken a run into Russia, " done " Switzerland and the Tyrol thoroughly and France and Germany and were soon going to Spain, and from there to Paris, to shop, in preparation for their return home in the spring.

" Of course we shall want quantities of things," she said. " No one will believe that we have been abroad unless we bring home a lot of clothes. The *lingerie* and all that is ordered already ; but the dresses must be made at the last moment, and we shall have a horrid time of it, I suppose. Worth has promised to make me two walking-suits and two ball-dresses, but he's very bad about keeping his word. Did you do much when you were in Paris, Katy ? "

" We went to the Louvre three times, and to Versailles and St. Cloud," said Katy, wilfully misunderstanding her.

" Oh, I didn't mean that kind of stupid thing ! I meant gowns. What did you buy ? "

" One tailor-made suit of dark-blue cloth."

" My ! What moderation ! "

Poor Lilly ! Europe to her was all " things." She had collected trunks full of objects to carry home, but of the other collections, which do not go into trunks, she had little or none. Her mind was as empty, her heart as untouched as ever; the beauty and the glory and the pathos of art and history and Nature had been poured out in vain before her closed and indifferent eyes.

Life soon dropped into a peaceful routine at the Pension Suisse, which was at the same time restful and stimulating. Katy's first act in the morning, as soon as she opened her eyes, was to hurry to the window in hopes of getting a glimpse of Corsica. She had discovered that this elusive island could almost always be seen from Nice at the dawning, but that as soon as the sun was fairly up, it vanished, to appear no more for the rest of the day. There was something fascinating to her imagination in the hovering mountain outline between sea and sky. She felt as if she were under an engagement to be there to meet it, and she rarely missed the appointment. Then, after

Corsica had pulled the bright mists over its face and melted from view, she would hurry with her dressing, and as soon as was practicable, set to work to make the *salon* look bright before the coffee and rolls should appear, a little after eight o'clock. Mrs. Ashe always found the fire lit, the little meal cosily set out beside it, and Katy's happy untroubled face to welcome her when she emerged from her room ; and the cheer of these morning repasts made a good beginning for the day.

Then came walking and a French lesson, and a long sitting on the beach, while Katy worked at her home letters and Amy raced up and down in the sun ; and then towards noon Lieutenant Ned generally appeared, and some scheme of pleasure was set on foot. Mrs. Ashe ignored his evident *penchant* for Lilly Page, and claimed his time and attention as hers by right. Young Worthington was a good deal "taken" with the pretty Lilly ; still, he had an old-time devotion for his sister and the habit of doing what she desired, and he yielded to her behests with no audible objections. He made a fourth in the carriage while they drove over the lovely hills which en- circle Nice towards the north, to Cimiers and the Val de St. André, or down the coast towards Ventimiglia. He went with them to Monte Carlo and Mentone, and was their escort again and again when they visited the great warships as they lay at anchor in a bay which in its translucent blue was like an enor- mous sapphire.

Mrs. Page and her daughter were included in these parties more than once ; but there was something in Mrs. Ashe's cool appropriation of her brother which was infinitely vexatious to Lilly, who before her arrival had rather looked upon Lieutenant Worthington as her own especial property.

"I wish *that* Mrs. Ashe had stayed at home," she told her mother. "She quite spoils everything. Mr. Worthington isn't half so nice as he was before she came. I do believe she has a plan for making him fall in love with Katy ; but there she makes a miss of it, for he doesn't seem to care anything about her."

"Katy is a nice girl enough," pronounced her mother, "but not of the sort to attract a gay young man, I should fancy. I don't believe *she* is thinking of any such thing. You needn't be afraid, Lilly."

"I'm not afraid," said Lilly, with a pout; "only it's so provoking!"

Mrs. Page was quite right. Katy was not thinking of any such thing. She liked Ned Worthington's frank manners; she owned, quite honestly, that she thought him handsome, and she particularly admired the sort of deferential affection which he showed to Mrs. Ashe, and his nice ways with Amy. For herself, she was aware that he scarcely noticed her except as politeness demanded that he should be civil to his sister's friend but the knowledge did not trouble her particularly. Her head was full of interesting things, plans, ideas. She was not accustomed to being made the object of admiration, and experienced none of the vexations of a neglected belle. If Lieutenant Worthington happened to talk to her, she responded frankly and freely; if he did not, she occupied herself with something else; in either case she was quite unembarrassed both in feeling and manner, and had none of the awkwardness which comes from disappointed vanity and baffled expectations, and the need for concealing them.

Towards the close of December the officers of the flagship gave a ball, which was the great event of the season to the gay world of Nice. Americans were naturally in the ascendant on an American frigate; and of all the American girls present, Lilly Page was unquestionably the prettiest. Exquisitely dressed in white lace, with bands of turquoise on her neck and arms and in her hair, she had more partners than she knew what to do with, more bouquets than she could well carry, and compliments enough to turn any girl's head. Thrown off her guard by her triumphs, she indulged a little vindictive feeling which had been growing in her mind of late on account of what she chose to consider certain derelictions of duty on the part of Lieutenant Worthington, and treated him to a taste of neglect. She was engaged three deep when he asked her to dance; she did not hear when he invited her to walk; she turned a cold shoulder when he tried to talk, and seemed absorbed by the other cavaliers, naval and otherwise, who crowded about her.

Piqued and surprised, Ned Worthington turned to Katy. She did not dance, saying frankly, that she did not know how, and was too tall; and she was rather simply dressed in a pearl-grey silk, which had been her best gown the winter before in Burnet, with a bunch of red roses in the white lace of the tucker, and another in her hand, both the gifts of little Amy; but she looked pleasant and serene, and there was something about her which somehow soothed his disturbed mind, as he offered her his arm for a walk on the decks.

For a while they said little, and Katy was quite content to pace up and down in silence, enjoying the really beautiful scene —the moonlight on the bay, the deep, wavering reflections of the dark hulls and slender spars, the fairy effect of the coloured lamps and lanterns, and the brilliant moving maze of the dancers.

" Do you care for this sort of thing? " he suddenly asked.

" What sort of thing do you mean? "

" Oh, all this jigging and waltzing and amusement! "

" I don't know how to ' jig,' but it's delightful to look on," she answered merrily. " I never saw anything so pretty in my life."

The happy tone of her voice, and the unruffled face which she turned upon him, quieted his irritation.

" I really believe you mean it," he said; " and yet, if you won't think me rude to say so, most girls would consider the thing dull enough if they were only getting out of it what you are—if they were not dancing, I mean, and nobody in particular was trying to entertain them."

" But everything *is* being done to entertain me," cried Katy. " I can't imagine what makes you think that it could seem dull. I am in it all, don't you see—I have my share—— Oh, I am stupid, I can't make you understand! "

" Yes, you do. I understand perfectly, I think; only it is such a different point of view from what girls in general would take." (By girls he meant Lilly!) " Please do not think me uncivil."

" You are not uncivil at all; but don't let us talk any more about me. Look at the lights between the shadows of the masts on the water. How they quiver! I never saw anything so beautiful, I think. And how warm it is! I can't believe that we are in December and that it is nearly Christmas."

" How is Polly going to celebrate her Christmas? Have you decided?"

" Amy is to have a Christmas tree for her dolls, and two other dolls are coming. We went out this morning to buy things for it—tiny little toys and candles fit for Lilliput. And that reminds me, do you suppose one can get any Christmas greens here?"

" Why not? The place seems full of green."

" That's just it; the summer looks makes it unnatural. But I should like some to dress the parlour with, if they could be had."

" I'll see what I can find, and send you a load."

I don't know why this very simple talk should have made an impression on Lieutenant Worthington's mind, but somehow he did not forget it.

" ' Don't let us talk any more about me '," he said to himself, that night when alone in his cabin. " I wonder how long it would be before the other one did anything to divert the talk from herself. Some time, I fancy." He smiled rather grimly as he unbuckled his sword-belt. It is unlucky for a girl when she starts a train of reflection like this. Lilly's little attempt to pique her admirer had somehow missed its mark.

Amy played on the beach the next afternoon, while Katy, in her favourite place on the beach, was at work on the long weekly letter which she never failed to send home to Burnet. She held her portfolio in her lap, and her pen ran rapidly over the paper.

She was suddenly interrupted by a crunching step on the gravel behind her.

" Good afternoon! " said a voice. " Polly has sent me to fetch you and Amy in. She says it is growing cool."

" We were just coming," said Katy, beginning to put away her papers.

Ned Worthington sat down on the cloak beside her. The distance was now steel grey against the sky; then came a stripe of violet, and then a broad sheet of the vivid iridescent blue which one sees on the necks of peacocks, which again melted into the long line of flashing surf.

" Are you going? " said Lieutenant Worthington in a tone of surprise, as she rose.

" Didn't you say that Polly wanted us to come in? "

" Why, yes ; but it seems too good to leave, doesn't it ?
Oh, by the way, Miss Carr, I came across a man to-day and
ordered your greens ! They will be sent on Christmas Eve. Is
that right ? "

" Quite right, and we are ever so much obliged to you." She
turned for a last look at the sea, and, unseen by Ned Worthington, formed her lips into a " good night." Katy had made
great friends with the Mediterranean.

The promised " greens " appeared on the afternoon before
Christmas Day, in the shape of an enormous fagot of laurel and
laurustinus and holly and box, orange and lemon boughs with
ripe fruit hanging from them, thick ivy tendrils whole yards
long, arbutus, pepper-tree, and great branches of acacia,
covered with feathery yellow bloom. The man apologised for
bringing so little. The gentleman had ordered two francs' worth,
he said, but this was all he could carry ; he would fetch some
more if the young lady wished. But Katy, exclaiming with
delight over her wealth, wished no more ; so the man departed,
and the three friends proceeded to turn the little *salon* into a
fairy bower. Every photograph and picture was wreathed in
ivy, long garlands hung on either side of the windows, and the
chimney-piece and door-frames became clustering banks of leaf
and blossom.

Mabel and Mary Matilda, and their two doll visitors, sat
gravely round the table, in the laps of their little mistresses ;
and Katy, putting on an apron and an improvised cap, and
speaking Irish very fast, served them with a repast of rolls and
cocoa, raspberry jam, and delicious little almond cakes. The
fun waxed fast and furious, and Lieutenant Worthington, coming in with his hands full of parcels for the Christmas tree, was
just in time to hear Katy remark in a strong County Kerry
brogue :

" Och, thin indade, Miss Amy, and it's no more cake you'll
be getting out of me the night. That's four pieces you've ate,
and it's little shlape your poor mother'll git with you a-tossin'
and tumblin' forenenst her all night long because of your big
appetite."

" Oh, Miss Katy, talk Irish some more ! " cried Amy.

" Is it Irish you'd be afther having me talk, when it's me own

langwidge, and sorrow a bit of another do I know?" demanded
Katy. Then she caught sight of the new arrival and stopped
short with a blush and a laugh.

"Come in, Mr. Worthington," she said; "we're at supper,
as you see, and I am acting as waitress."

"Oh, Uncle Ned, please go away," pleaded Amy, "or Katy
will be polite, and not talk Irish any more!"

"Indade, and the less ye say about politeness the bether,
when ye're afther ordering the jantleman out of the room in
that fashion!" said the waitress. Then she pulled off her cap
and untied her apron.

"Now for the Christmas tree," she said.

It was a very little tree, but it bore some remarkable fruits;
for in addition to the "tiny toys and candles fit for Lilliput,"
various parcels were found to have been hastily added at the
last moment for various people. The *Natchitoches* had lately
come from the Levant, and delightful Oriental confections now
appeared for Amy and Mrs. Ashe; Turkish slippers, all gold
embroidery; towels, with richly decorated ends in silks and
tinsel;—all the pretty superfluities which the East holds out to
charm gold from the pockets of her Western visitors. A pretty
little dagger in agate and silver fell to Katy's share out of what
Lieutenant Worthington called his "loot"; and, besides, a
most beautiful specimen of the inlaid work for which Nice is
famous—a looking-glass, with a stand and little doors to close
it in—which was a present from Mrs. Ashe. It was quite unlike a Christmas Eve at home, but altogether delightful; and
as Katy sat next morning on the sand, after service in the
English church, to finish her home letter, and felt the sun warm
on her cheek, and the perfumed air blow past as softly as in
June, she had to remind herself that Christmas is not necessarily
synonymous with snow and winter, but means the great central
heat and warmth, the advent of Him who came to lighten the
whole earth.

A few days after this pleasant Christmas they left Nice. All
of them felt a reluctance to move, and Amy loudly bewailed the
necessity.

"If I could stay here till it is time to go home, I shouldn't be
home-sick at all," she declared.

" But what a pity it would be not to see Italy ! " said her mother. " Think of Naples and Rome and Venice ! "

" I don't want to think about them. It makes me feel as if I was studying a great long geography lesson, and it tires me so to learn it."

" Amy, dear, you're not well."

" Yes I am—quite well ; only I don't want to go away from Nice."

" You only have to learn a little bit at a time of your geography lesson, you know," suggested Katy ; " and it's a great deal nicer way to study it than out of a book." But though she spoke cheerfully she was conscious that she shared Amy's reluctance.

" It's all laziness," she told herself. " Nice has been so pleasant that it has spoiled me."

The next day brought them to Genoa, to a hotel once the stately palace of an archbishop, where they were lodged, all three together, in an enormous room, so high and broad and long that their three little curtained beds, set behind a screen of carved wood, made no impression on the space. There were no less than four sofas and double that number of arm-chairs in the room, besides a couple of monumental wardrobes ; but, as Katy remarked, several grand pianos could still have been moved in without anybody's feeling crowded. On one side of them lay the port of Genoa, filled with crafts from all parts of the world, and flying the flags of a dozen different nations. From the other they caught glimpses of the magnificent old city, rising in tier over tier of churches and palaces and gardens ; while nearer still were narrow streets, which glittered with gold filigree and the shops of jewel-workers. And while they went in and out, and gazed and wondered, Lilly Page, at the Pension Suisse, was saying :

" I am so glad that Katy and *that* Mrs. Ashe are gone ! Nothing has been so pleasant since they came. Lieutenant Worthington is dreadfully stiff and stupid, and seems quite different from what he used to be. But now that we have got rid of them it will all come right again."

" I really don't think Katy was to blame," said Mrs. Page. " She never seemed to me to be making any effort to attract him."

" Oh, Katy is sly ! " responded Lilly vindictively. " She never *seems* to do anything, but somehow she always gets her own way. I suppose she thought I didn't see her keeping him down there on the beach the other day when he was coming in to call on us, but I did. It was just out of spite, and because she wanted to vex me ; I know it was."

" Well, dear, she's gone now, and you won't be worried with her again," said her mother soothingly. " Don't pout so, Lilly, and wrinkle up your forehead. It's very unbecoming."

" Yes, she's gone," snapped Lilly ; " and as she's bound for the east, and we for the west, we are not likely to meet again, for which I am devoutly thankful."

CHAPTER VIII

ON THE TRACK OF ULYSSES

" WE ARE going to follow the track of Ulysses," said Katy, with her eyes fixed on the little travelling-map in her guide-book. " Do you realise that, Polly dear ? He and his companions sailed these very seas before us, and we shall see the sights they saw— Circe's Cape and the Isles of the Sirens, and Polyphemus himself, perhaps—who knows ? "

The *Marco Polo* had just cast off her moorings, and was slowly steaming out of the crowded port of Genoa into the heart of a still rosy sunset. The water was perfectly smooth ; no motion could be felt but the engine's throb. The trembling foam of the long wake showed glancing points of phosphorescence here and there, while low on the eastern sky a great silver planet burned like a signal-lamp.

" Polly dear," said Katy, who was in the highest spirits. " There is one delightful thing I forgot to tell you about ! The captain says we shall stay in Leghorn all day to-morrow and we shall have plenty of time to run up to Pisa and see the Cathedral and the Leaning Tower. Now, that is something Ulysses didn't do ! I am so glad I didn't die of measles when I was little, as Rose Red used to say ! " She gave her book a toss

into the air as she spoke, and caught it again as it fell, very much
as the Katy Carr of twelve years ago might have done.

"What a child you are!" said Mrs. Ashe approvingly;
"you never seem out of sorts or tired of things."

"Out of sorts! I should think not! And pray why should I
be, Polly dear?"

Katy had taken to calling her friend "Polly dear" of late—
a trick picked up half-unconsciously from Lieutenant Ned. Mrs.
Ashe liked it; it was sisterly and intimate, she said, and made
her feel nearer Katy's age.

"Does the tower really lean?" questioned Amy—"far over,
I mean, so that we can see it?"

"We shall know to-morrow," replied Katy. "If it doesn't,
I shall lose all my confidence in human nature."

Katy's confidence in human nature was not doomed to be
impaired. There stood the famous tower, when they reached the
Place del Duomo in Pisa, next morning, looking all aslant,
exactly as it does in the pictures and the alabaster models, and
seeming as if in another moment it must topple over, from its
own weight, upon their heads. Mrs. Ashe declared that it was
so unnatural that it made her flesh creep; and when she was
coaxed up the winding staircase to the top, she turned so giddy
that they were all thankful to get her safely down to firm
ground again. She turned her back upon the tower, as they
crossed the grassy space to the majestic old Cathedral, saying
that if she thought about it any more, she should become a dis-
believer in the attraction of gravitation, which she had always
been told all respectable people *must* believe in.

The guide showed them the lamp, swinging by a long, slender
chain, before which Galileo is said to have sat and pondered
while he worked out his theory of the pendulum. This lamp
seemed a sort of own cousin to the attraction of gravitation, and
they gazed upon it with respect. Then they went to the Bap-
tistery to see Niccolo Pisano's magnificent pulpit of creamy
marble, a mass of sculpture supported on the backs of lions, and
the equally lovely font, and to admire the extraordinary sound
which their guide evoked from a mysterious echo, with which
he seemed to be on intimate terms, for he made it say whatever
he would, and almost "answer back."

Their way to the hotel where they were to lunch led them through a narrow street inhabited by the poorer classes—a dusty street with high shabby buildings on either side and wide doorways giving glimpses of interior courtyards. As is usual in poor streets, there were swarms of children ; and the appearance of little Amy with her long bright hair falling over her shoulders, and Mabel clasped in her arms, created a great sensation. The children in the street shouted and exclaimed, and other children within the houses heard the sounds and came trooping out. The very air seemed full of eager faces and little brown and curly heads bobbing up and down with excitement, and black eyes fixed upon big beautiful Mabel, who with her thick wig of flaxen hair, her blue velvet dress and jacket, feathered hat and little muff, seemed to them like some strange small marvel from another world. They could not decide whether she was a living child or a make-believe one, but they dared not come near enough to find out ; so they clustered at a little distance, pointed with their fingers, and whispered and giggled, while Amy, much pleased with the admiration shown for her darling, lifted Mabel up to view.

At last one droll little girl with a white cap on her round head seemed to make up her mind, and, darting indoors, returned with *her* doll—a poor little image of wood, its only garment a coarse shirt of red cotton. This she held out for Amy to see. Amy smiled for the first time since meeting the children and Katy, taking Mabel from her, made signs that the two dolls should kiss each other. But though the little Italian screamed with laughter at the idea of a *bacio* between two dolls, she would by no means allow it, and hid her treasure behind her back, blushing and giggling, and saying something very fast which none of them understood, while she waved two fingers at them with a curious gesture.

" I do believe she is afraid Mabel will cast the evil eye on her doll," said Katy at last, with a sudden understanding as to what this pantomime meant.

" Why, you silly thing," cried the outraged Amy ; " do you suppose for one moment that my child could hurt your dirty old dolly ? You ought to be glad to have her noticed at all by anybody that's clean."

The sound of the foreign tongue completed the discomfiture of the little Italian. With a shriek she fled, and all the other children after her; pausing at a distance to look back at the alarming creatures who didn't speak the familiar language. Katy, wishing to leave a pleasant impression, made Mabel kiss her waxen fingers towards them. This sent the children off into another fit of laughter and chatter, and they followed our friends for quite a distance as they proceeded on their way to the hotel.

All that night, over a sea as smooth as glass, the *Marco Polo* slipped along the coasts past which the ships of Ulysses sailed in those old legendary days which wear so charmed a light to our modern eyes. Katy roused at three in the morning, and, looking from her cabin window, had a glimpse of an island, which her map showed her must be Elba, where that war-eagle Napoleon was chained for a while. Then she fell asleep again, and when she roused in full daylight the steamer was off the coast of Ostia and nearing the mouth of the Tiber. Dreamy mountain-shapes rose beyond the far-away Campagna, and every curve and every indentation of the coast bore a name which recalled some interesting thing.

About eleven a dim-drawn bubble appeared on the horizon, which the captain assured them was the dome of St. Peter's, nearly thirty miles distant. This was one of the " moments " which Clover had been fond of speculating about ; and Katy, contrasting the real with the imaginary moment, could not help smiling. Neither she nor Clover had ever supposed that her first glimpse of the great dome was to be so little impressive.

That night, the *Marco Polo* sailed into the Bay of Naples, past Vesuvius, whose dusky curl of smoke could be seen outlined against the luminous sky, and brought her passengers to their landing-place.

They woke next morning to a summer atmosphere full of yellow sunshine and true July warmth. Flower-vendors stood on every corner, and pursued each newcomer with their fragrant wares. Katy could not stop exclaiming over the cheapness of the flowers, which were thrust in at the carriage windows as they drove slowly up and down the streets. They were tied into flat nosegays, whose centre was a white camellia, encircled with concentric rows of pink tea-rosebuds, ring after ring, till the whole was the size of an ordinary milk-pan; all to be had for the sum of ten cents! But after they had bought two or three of these enormous bouquets, and had discovered that not a single rose boasted an inch of stem, and that all were pierced with long wires through their very hearts, she ceased to care for them.

" I would rather have one Souvenir or General Jaqueminot, with a long stem and plenty of leaves, than a dozen of these stiff platters of bouquets," Katy told Mrs. Ashe. But when they drove beyond the city gates, and the coachman came to anchor beneath walls overhung with the same roses, and she found that she might stand on the seat and pull down as many branches of the lovely flowers as she desired, and gather wallflowers for herself out of the clefts in the masonry, she was entirely satisfied.

" This is the Italy of my dreams," she said.

With all its beauty there was an underlying sense of danger about Naples, which interfered with their enjoyment of it. Evil smells came in at the windows, or confronted them as they went about the city. There seemed something deadly in the air. Whispered reports met their ears of cases of fever, which the landlords of the hotels were doing their best to hush up. An American gentleman was said to be lying very ill at one house. A lady had died the week before at another. Mrs. Ashe grew nervous.

" We will just take a rapid look at a few of the principal things," she told Katy, " and then get away as fast as we can. Amy is so on my mind that I have no peace of my life. I keep feeling her pulse and imagining that she does not look right; and though I know it is all my fancy, I am impatient to be off. You won't mind, will you, Katy? "

After that everything they did was done in a hurry. Katy felt as if she were being driven about by a cyclone, as they rushed from one sight to another, filling up all the chinks between with shopping, which was irresistible where everything was so pretty and so wonderfully cheap. She herself purchased a tortoise-shell fan and chain for Rose Red, and had her monogram carved upon it; a coral locket for Elsie; some studs for Dorry; and for her father a small, beautiful vase of bronze, copied from one of the Pompeian antiques.

" How charming it is to have money to spend in such a place as this ! " she said to herself, with a sigh of satisfaction, as she surveyed these delightful buyings. " I only wish I could get ten times as many things and take them to ten times as many people. Papa was so wise about it ! I can't think how it is that he always knows beforehand exactly how people are going to feel, and what they will want ! "

Mrs. Ashe also bought a great many things for herself and Amy, and to take home as presents ; and it was all very pleasant and satisfactory, except for that subtle sense of danger from which they could not escape and which made them glad to go. " See Naples and die," says the old adage ; and the saying has proved sadly true in the case of many an American traveller.

Besides the talk of fever there was also a good deal of gossip about brigands going about, as is generally the case in Naples and its vicinity. Something was said to have happened to a party on one of the heights above Sorrento ; and though nobody knew exactly what the something was, or was willing to vouch for the story, Mrs. Ashe and Katy felt a good deal of trepidation as they entered the carriage which was to take them to the neighbourhood where the mysterious " something " had occurred.

It is a pity that the beautiful drive should have been wasted on Mrs. Ashe and Katy, but they were too frightened to half enjoy it. Their carriage was driven by a shaggy young savage, who looked quite wild enough to be a bandit himself. He cracked his whip loudly as they rolled along, and every now and then gave a long shrill whistle. Mrs. Ashe was sure that these were signals to his band, who were lurking somewhere on the olive-hung hillsides. She thought she detected him once or twice making signs to certain questionable-looking characters as they passed ; and she fancied that the people they met gazed at them with an air of commiseration, as upon victims who were being carried to execution. Her fears affected Katy ; so, though they talked and laughed, and made jokes to amuse Amy, who must not be scared or led to suppose that anything was amiss, and to the outward view seemed a very merry party, they were privately quaking in their shoes all the way, and enjoying a deal of highly superfluous misery. And after all they reached Sorrento in perfect safety; and the driver, who looked so dangerous, turned out to be a respectable young man, with a wife and family to support, who considered a plateful of macaroni and a glass of sour red wine as the height of luxury, and was grateful for a small gratuity of thirty cents or so, which would enable him to purchase these dainties. Mrs. Ashe had a very bad headache next day, to pay for her fright; but she and Katy agreed that they had been very foolish, and resolved to pay no more attention to unaccredited rumours or allow them to spoil their enjoyment, which was a sensible resolution to make.

Their hotel was perched directly over the sea. From the balcony of their sitting-room they looked down a sheer cliff some sixty feet high, into the water; their bedrooms opened on a garden of roses, with an orange grove beyond. Not far from them was the great gorge which cuts the little town of Sorrento almost in two, and whose seaward end makes the harbour of the place. Katy was never tired of peering down into this strange and beautiful cleft, whose sides, two hundred feet in depth, are hung with vines and trailing growths of all sorts, and seem all a-tremble with the fairy fronds of maidenhair ferns growing out of every chink and crevice.

They made two different excursions to Pompeii, which is within easy distance of Sorrento. They scrambled on donkeys over the hills, and had glimpses of the far-away Calabrian shore, of the natural arch, and the temples of Pæstum shining in the sun many miles distant. On Katy's birthday, which fell towards the end of January, Mrs. Ashe let her have her choice of a treat; and she elected to go to the Island of Capri, which none of them had seen. It turned out a perfect day, with sea and wind exactly right for the sail, and for getting into the famous "Blue Grotto," which can only be entered under particular conditions of tide and weather. And they climbed the great cliff-rise at the island's end, and saw the ruins of the villa built by the wicked emperor Tiberius, and the awful place known as his "Leap," down which, it is said, he made his victims throw themselves; and they lunched at a hotel which bore his name, and just at sunset pushed off again for the row home over the charmed sea. This return voyage was almost the pleasantest thing of all the day. The water was smooth, the moon at its full.

It was larger and more brilliant than American moons are, and seemed to possess an actual warmth and colour. The boatmen timed their oar-strokes to the cadence of Neopolitan *barcaroles* and folk-songs, full of rhythmic movement, which seemed caught from the pulsing tides. And when at last the bow grated on the sands of the Sorrento landing-place, Katy drew a long, regretful breath, and declared that this was her best birthday-gift of all, better than Amy's flowers, or the pretty tortoise-shell locket that Mrs. Ashe had given her, better even than the letter from home, which, timed by happy accident, had arrived by the morning's post to make a bright opening for the day.

But all pleasant things must come to an end.

" Katy," said Mrs. Ashe, one afternoon in early February, " I heard some ladies talking just now in the *salon*, and they said that Rome is filling up very fast. The Carnival begins in less than two weeks, and everybody wants to be there then. If we don't make haste we shall not be able to get any rooms."

" Oh dear ! " said Katy, " it is very trying not to be able to be in two places at once. I want to see Rome dreadfully, and yet I cannot bear to leave Sorrento. We have been very happy here, haven't we ? "

So they took up their wandering staves again, and departed for Rome, like the Apostle, " not knowing what should befall them there."

CHAPTER IX

A ROMAN HOLIDAY

" OH dear ! " said Mrs. Ashe, as she folded her letters and laid them aside, " I wish those Pages would go away from Nice, or else that the frigates were not there."

" Why, what's the matter ? " asked Katy, looking up from the many-leaved journal from Clover over which she was poring.

" Nothing is the matter except that those everlasting people haven't gone to Spain yet, as they said they would, and Ned seems to keep on seeing them," replied Mrs. Ashe petulantly.

" But, dear Polly, what difference does it make ? And they never did promise you to go at any particular time, did they ? "

" N-o, they didn't ; but I wish they would, all the same. Not that Ned is such a goose as really to care anything for that foolish Lilly ! " Then she gave a little laugh at her own inconsistency, and added : " But I oughtn't to abuse her when she is your cousin."

" Don't mention it," said Katy cheerfully. " But, really, I don't see why poor Lilly need worry you so, Polly dear."

The room in which this conversation took place was on the very topmost floor of the Hotel del Mondo in Rome. It was large and many-windowed ; and though there was a little bed in one corner half-hidden behind a calico screen, with a bureau and washing-stand, and a sort of stout mahogany hat-tree on which Katy's dresses and jackets were hanging, the remaining space, with a sofa and easy-chairs grouped round a fire, and a round table furnished with books and a lamp, was ample enough to make a good substitute for the private sitting-room which Mrs. Ashe had not been able to procure on account of the near approach of the Carnival and the consequent crowding of strangers to Rome. In fact, she was assured that under the circumstances she was lucky in finding rooms as good as these ; and she made the most of the assurance as a consolation for the somewhat unsatisfactory food and service of the hotel, and the four long flights of stairs which must be passed every time they needed to reach the dining-room or the street door.

The party had been in Rome only four days, but already they had seen a host of interesting things. They had stood in the strange sunken space with its marble floor and broken columns, which is all that is left of the great Roman Forum. They had visited the Colosseum, at that period still overhung with ivy garlands and trailing greeneries, and not, as now, scraped clean and bare and " tidied " out of much of its picturesqueness. They had seen the Baths of Caracalla and the Temple of Janus and St. Peter's and the Vatican Marbles, and had driven out on the Campagna and to the Pamphili-Doria Villa to gather purple and red anemones, and to the English cemetery to see the grave of Keats. They had also peeped into certain shops, and attended a reception at the American Minister's—in short, like most unwarned travellers, they had done about twice as much as prudence and experience would have permitted, had those worthies been consulted.

All the romance of Katy's nature responded to the fascination of the ancient city—the capital of the world, as it may truly be called. The shortest drive or walk brought them face to face with innumerable and unexpected delights. No matter what it was,—a bit of oddly-tinted masonry with a tuft of brown and orange wallflowers hanging upon it, or a vegetable stall where endive and chicory and curly lettuces were arranged in wreaths with tiny orange gourds and scarlet peppers for points of colour, it was all Rome, and, by virtue of that word, different from any other place—more suggestive, more interesting, ten times more mysterious than any other could possibly be, so Katy thought.

This fact consoled her for everything and anything—for the fleas, the dirt, for the queer things they had to eat and the still queerer odours they were forced to smell ! Nothing seemed of any particular consequence except the deep sense of enjoyment, and the newly-discovered world of thought and sensation of which she had become suddenly conscious.

The only drawback to her happiness as the days went on, was that little Amy did not seem quite well or like herself. She had taken a cold on the journey from Naples, and though it did not seem serious, that, or something, made her look pale and thin. Her mother said she was growing fast ; but the explanation did not quite account for the wistful look in the child's eyes and the tired feeling of which she continually complained. Mrs. Ashe, with vague uneasiness, began to talk of cutting short their Roman stay and getting Amy off to the more bracing air of Florence. But meanwhile there was the Carnival close at hand, which they must by no means lose ; and the feeling that their opportunity might be a brief one made her and Katy all the more anxious to make the very most of their time. So they filled the days full with sights to see and things to do, and came and went ; sometimes taking Amy with them, but more often leaving her at the hotel under the care of a kind German chambermaid, who spoke pretty good English and to whom Amy had taken a fancy.

The roof, which Amy had chosen as a play-place, covered the whole of the great hotel, and had been turned into a sort of upper-air garden by the simple process of gravelling it all over, placing trellises of ivy here and there, and setting tubs of oranges and oleanders and boxes of gay geraniums and stock-gilly-flowers on the balustrades. A tame fawn was tethered there. Amy adopted him as a playmate; and what with his company and that of the flowers, the times when her mother and Katy were absent from her passed not unhappily.

Katy always repaired to the roof as soon as they came in from their long mornings and afternoons of sightseeing. Years afterwards, she would remember with contrition how pathetic-ally glad Ann always was to see her. She would put her little head on Katy's breast and hold her tight for many minutes without saying a word. When she did speak it was always about the house and the garden that she talked. She never asked any questions as to where Katy had been, or what she had done; it seemed to tire her to think about it.

" I should be very lonely sometimes if it were not for my dear little fawn," she told Katy once. " He is so sweet that I don't miss you and mamma very much while I have him to play with. I call him Florio—don't you think that is a pretty name? I like to stay with him a great deal better than to go about with you to those nasty-smelling old churches, with fleas hopping all over them! "

So Amy was left in peace with her fawn, and the others made haste to see all they could before the time came to go to Florence.

Katy realised one of the " moments " for which she had come to Europe when she stood for the first time on the balcony overhanging the Corso, which Mrs. Ashe had hired in company with some acquaintances made at the hotel, and looked down at the ebb and surge of the just-begun Carnival. The narrow street seemed humming with people of all sorts and conditions. Some were masked, some were not. There was ladies and gentlemen in fashionable clothes, peasants in the gayest costumes, sur-prised-looking tourists in tall hats and linen dusters, harlequins, clowns, devils, nuns, dominoes of every colour—red, white, blue, black; while above, the balconies bloomed like a rose-garden with pretty faces framed in lace veils or picturesque hats. Flowers were everywhere wreathed along the house-fronts, tied to the horses' ears, in ladies' hands and gentlemen's button-holes, while vendors went up and down the street bearing great trays of violets and carnations and camellias for sale. The air was full of cries and laughter, and the shrill calls of merchants advertising their wares—candy, fruit, birds, lanterns, and *confetti*, the latter being merely lumps of lime, large or small, with a pea or a bean embedded in each lump to give it weight. Boxes full of this unpleasant confection were suspended in front of each balcony, with tin scoops to use in ladling it out and flinging it about. Everybody wore or carried a wire mask as protection against this white, incessant shower, and before long the air became full of a fine dust, which hung above the Corso like a mist, and filled the eyes and noses and clothes of all present with irritating particles.

Pasquino's Car was passing underneath just as Katy and Mrs. Ashe arrived—a gorgeous affair, hung with silken draperies, and bearing as symbol an enormous egg in which the Carnival was supposed to be in act of incubation. A huge wagon followed in its wake, on which was a house some sixteen feet square, whose sole occupant was a gentleman attended by five servants, who kept him supplied with *confetti*, which he showered liberally on the heads of the crowd. Then came a car in the shape of a steamboat, with a smoke-pipe and sails, over which flew the Union Jack, and which was manned with a party wearing the dress of British tars. The next wagon bore a company of jolly maskers equipped with many-coloured bladders, which they banged and rattled as they went along. Following this was a troupe of beautiful circus-horses, cream-coloured with scarlet trappings, or sorrel with blue, ridden by ladies in pale-green velvet laced with silver or blue velvet and gold. Another car bore a bird-cage which was an exact imitation of St. Peter's, within which perched a lonely old parrot. This device evidently had a political signification, for it was alternately hissed and applauded as it went along. The whole scene was like a brilliant, rapidly-shifting dream; and Katy, as she stood with lips apart and eyes wide open with wonderment and pleasure, forgot whether she was in the body or not—forgot everything except what was passing before her gaze.

Exactly opposite them was a balcony hung with white silk, in which sat a lady who seemed to be of some distinction; for every now and then an officer in brilliant uniform, or some official covered with orders, and stars, would be shown in by her servants, bow before her with the utmost deference, and after a little conversation retire, kissing her gloved hand as he went. The lady was a beautiful person, with lustrous black eyes and dark hair, over which a lace mantilla was fastened with diamond stars. She wore pale-blue with white flowers, and altogether, as Katy afterwards wrote to Clover, reminded her exactly of one of those beautiful princesses whom they used to play about in their childhood and quarrel over, because every one of them wanted to be the Princess and nobody else.

" I wonder who she is," said Mrs. Ashe in a low tone. " She might be almost anybody from her looks. She keeps glancing across to us, Katy. Do you know, I think she has taken a fancy to you."

Perhaps the lady had ; for just then she turned her head and said a word to one of her footmen, who immediately placed something in her hand. It was a little shining bonbonnière, and, rising, she threw it straight at Katy. Alas, it struck the edge of the balcony and fell into the street below, where it was picked up by a ragged little peasant girl in a red jacket, who raised a pair of astonished eyes to the heavens, as if sure that the gift must have fallen straight from thence. Katy bent forward to watch its fate, and went through a little pantomime of regret and despair for the benefit of the opposite lady, who only laughed, and, taking another from her servant, flung with better aim, so that it fell exactly at Katy's feet. This was a gilded box in the shape of a mandolin, with sugar-plums tucked cunningly away inside. Katy kissed both her hands in acknowledgement for the pretty toy, and tossed back a bunch of roses which she happened to be wearing in her dress. After that it seemed the chief amusement of the fair unknown to throw bonbons at Katy. Some went straight and some did not ; but before the afternoon ended, Katy had quite a lapful of confections and trifles—roses, sugared almonds, a satin casket, a silvered box in the shape of a horse-shoe, a tiny cage with orange blossoms for birds on the perches, a minute gondola with a *marron glacée* by way of passenger, and, prettiest of all, a little ivory harp strung with enamelled violets instead of wires. For all these favours she had nothing better to offer, in return, than a few long-tailed bonbons with gay streamers of ribbon. These the lady opposite caught very cleverly, rarely missing one, and kissing her hands in thanks each time.

" Isn't she exquisite ? " demanded Katy, her eyes shining with excitement. " Did you ever see anyone so lovely in your life, Polly, dear ? I never did. There, now! She is buying those birds to set them free, I do believe."

It was indeed so. A vendor of larks had, by the aid of a long staff, thrust a cage full of wretched little prisoners up into the balcony ; and " Katy's lady," as Mrs. Ashe called her, was paying for the whole. As they watched she opened the cage door and with the sweetest look on her face encouraged the birds to fly away. The poor little creatures cowered and hesitated, not knowing at first what use to make of their new liberty ; but at last one, the boldest of the company, hopped to the door, and with a glad, exultant chirp flew straight upwards. Then the others, taking courage from this example, followed, and all were lost to view in the twinkling of an eye.

" Oh, you angel ! " cried Katy, leaning over the edge of the balcony and kissing both hands impulsively. " I never saw any-one so sweet as you are in my life. Polly dear, I think carnivals are the most perfectly bewitching things in the world. How glad I am that this lasts a week, and that we can come every day ! Won't Amy be delighted with these bonbons ! I do hope my lady will be here to-morrow."

How little she dreamed that she was never to enter that balcony again ! How little can any of us see what lies before us till it comes so near that we cannot help seeing it, or shut our eyes, or turn away !

The next morning, almost as soon as it was light, Mrs. Ashe tapped at Katy's door. She was in her dressing-gown, and her eyes looked large and frightened.

" Amy is ill," she cried. " She has been hot and feverish all night, and she says that her head aches dreadfully. What shall I do, Katy? We ought to have a doctor at once, and I don't know the name even of any doctor here."

Katy sat up in bed, and for one bewildered moment did not speak. Her brain felt in a whirl of confusion; but presently it cleared, and she saw what to do.

"I will write a note to Mrs. Sands," she said. Mrs. Sands was the wife of the American Minister, and one of the few acquaintances they had made since they came to Rome. "You remember how nice she was the other day, and how we liked her; and she has lived here so long that of course she must know all about the doctors. Don't you think that is the best thing to do?"

"The very best," said Mrs. Ashe, looking relieved. "I wonder I did not think of it myself, but I am so confused that I can't think. Write the note at once, please, dear Katy. I will ring your bell for you, and then I must hurry back to Amy."

Katy made haste with the note. The answer came promptly in half an hour, and by ten o'clock the physician recommended appeared. Dr. Hilary was a dark little Italian to all appearance; but his mother had been a Scotchwoman, and he spoke English very well—a great comfort to poor Mrs. Ashe, who knew not a word of Italian and not a great deal of French. He felt Amy's pulse for a long time, and took her temperature; but he gave no positive opinion, only left a prescription, and said that he would call later in the day, and should then be able to judge more clearly what the attack was likely to prove.

Katy augured ill from this reserve. There was no talk of going to the Carnival that afternoon; no one had any heart for it. Instead, Katy spent the time in trying to recollect all she had ever heard about the care of sick people.

All night Amy grew worse, and when Dr. Hilary came next day, he was forced to utter plainly the dreaded words "Roman fever." Amy was in for an attack—a light one he hoped it might be—but they had better know the truth and make ready for it.

Mrs. Ashe was utterly overwhelmed by this verdict, and for the first bewildered moments did not know which way to turn. Katy, happily, kept a steadier head. She had the advantage of a little preparation of thought, and had decided beforehand what it would be necessary to do " in case." Oh, that fateful " in case " ! The doctor and she consulted together, and the result was that Katy sought out the *padrona* of the establishment, and without hinting at the nature of Amy's attack, secured some rooms just vacated, which were at the end of a corridor, and a little removed from the rooms of other people. There was a large room with corner windows, a smaller one opening from it, and another, still smaller, close by, which would serve as a storeroom or might do for the use of a nurse.

When all was ready, Amy, well wrapped in her coverings, was carried down the entry and laid in the fresh bed with soft pillows about her ; and Katy, as she went to and fro, conveying clothes and books and filling drawers, felt that they were per- haps making arrangements for a long, hard trial of faith and spirits.

By the next day the necessity of a nurse became apparent, and in the afternoon Katy started out in a little hired carriage in search of one. She had a list of names, and went first to the English nurses ; but, finding them all engaged, she ordered the coachman to drive to a convent where there was hope that a nursing-sister might be procured.

Their route lay across the Corso. So utterly had the Carnival with all its gay follies vanished from her mind that she was for a moment astonished at finding herself entangled in a motley crowd, so dense that the coachman was obliged to rein in his horses and stand still for some time.

There were the same masks and dominoes, the same pictur- esque peasant costumes which had struck her as so gay and pretty only three days before. The same jests and merry laughter filled the air, but somehow it all seemed out of tune. The sense of cold, lonely fear that had taken possession of her killed all capacity for merriment ; the apprehension and solici- tude of which her heart was full made the gay chattering and squeaking of the crowd sound harsh and unfeeling. The bright colours affronted her dejection ; she did not want to see them. She lay back in the carriage, trying to be patient under the detention, and half shut her eyes.

A shower of lime-dust aroused her. It came from a party of

burly figures in white cotton dominoes, whose carriage had been stayed by the crowd close to her own. She signified by gestures that she had no *confetti* and no protection, that she " was not playing," in fact; but her appeal made no difference. The maskers kept on shovelling lime all over her hair and person and the carriage and never tired of the sport till an opportune break in the procession enabled their vehicle to move on.

The convent was propitious, and promised to send a sister next morning, with the proviso that every second day she was to come back to sleep and rest. Katy was too thankful for any aid to make objections, and drove home with visions of saintly nuns with pure, pale faces full of peace and resignation, such as she had read of in books, floating before her eyes.

Sister Ambrogia, when she appeared next day, did not exactly realise these imaginations. She was a plump little person, with rosy cheeks, a pair of demure black eyes, and a very obstinate mouth and chin. It soon appeared that natural inclination, combined with the rules of her convent, made her theory of a nurse's duties a very limited one.

In fact, all that Sister Ambrogia seemed able or willing to do, beyond the bathing of Amy's face and brushing her hair, which she accomplished handily, was to sit by the bedside telling her rosary, or plying a little ebony shuttle in the manufacture of a long strip of tatting. Even this amount of usefulness was interfered with by the fact that Amy, who by this time was in a semi-delirious condition, had taken an aversion to her at the first glance, and was not willing to be left with her for a single moment.

" I won't stay here alone with Sister Embroidery," she would cry, if her mother and Katy went into the next room for a moment's rest or a private consultation; " I hate Sister Embroidery! Come back, Mamma, come back this moment! She's making faces at me, and chattering just like an old parrot, and I don't understand a word she says. Take Sister Embroidery away, Mamma, I tell you! Don't you hear me? Come back, I say!"

The little voice would be raised to a shrill scream; and Mrs. Ashe and Katy, hurrying back, would find Amy sitting up on her pillow with wet, scarlet-flushed cheeks and eyes bright with fever, ready to throw herself out of bed ; while, calm as Mabel, whose curly head lay on the pillow beside her little mistress, Sister Ambrogia, unaware of the intricacies of the English language, was placidly telling her beads and muttering prayers to herself. Some of these prayers, I do not doubt, related to Amy's recovery, if not to her conversion, and were well meant ; but they were rather irritating under the circumstances !

CHAPTER X

CLEAR SHINING AFTER RAIN

WHEN the first shock is over and the inevitable realised and accepted, those who tend a long illness are apt to fall into a routine of life which helps to make the days seem short. The apparatus of nursing is got together. Every day the same things need to be done at the same hours and in the same way. Each little appliance is kept at hand ; and, sad and tired as the watchers may be, the very monotony and regularity of their proceedings give a certain stay for their thoughts to rest upon.

But there was little of this monotony to help Mrs. Ashe and Katy through with Amy's illness. Small chance was there for regularity of exact system ; for something unexpected was always turning up, and needful things were often lacking. The most ordinary comforts of the sick-room, or what are considered so in America, were hard to come by, and much of Katy's time was spent in devising substitutes to take their places.

Was ice needed ? A pailful of dirty snow would be brought in, full of straws, sticks, and other refuse, which had apparently been scraped from the surface of the street after a frosty night. Not a particle of it could be put into milk or water ; all that could be done was to make the pail serve the purpose of a refrigerator, and set bowls and tumblers in it to chill.

But the greatest trial of all was the beef-tea. It was Amy's sole food, and almost her only medicine ; for Dr. Hilary believed in leaving Nature pretty much to herself in cases of fever. The kitchen of the hotel sent up, under that name, a mixture of grease and hot water, which could not be given to Amy at all. In vain Katy remonstrated and explained the process. In vain did she go to the kitchen herself to translate a carefully-written recipe to the cook, and to slip a shining five-franc piece in his hand, which, it was hoped, would quicken his energies and soften his heart. In vain did she order private supplies of the best of beef from a separate market. The cooks stole the beef and ignored the recipe ; and day after day the same bottleful of greasy liquid came upstairs, which Amy would not touch, and which would have done her no good had she swallowed it all. At last, driven to desperation, Katy procured a couple of stout bottles, and every morning slowly and carefully cut up two pounds of meat into small pieces, sealed the bottle with her own seal ring, and sent it down to be boiled for a specified time. This answered better, for the thieving cook dared not tamper with her seal ; but it was a long and toilsome process, and consumed more time than she well knew how to spare—for there were continual errands to be done which no one could attend to but herself, and the interminable flights of stairs taxed her strength painfully, and seemed to grow longer and harder every day.

At last a good Samaritan turned up in the shape of an American lady with a house of her own who, hearing of their plight from Mrs. Sands, undertook to send each day a supply of strong, perfectly-made beef-tea from her own kitchen for Amy's use. It was an inexpressible relief, and the lightening of this one particular care made all the rest seem easier of endurance.

Another great relief came, when, after some delay, Dr. Hilary succeeded in getting an English nurse to take the places of the unsatisfactory Sister Ambrogia and her substitute, Sister Agatha, whom Amy, in her half-comprehending condition, persisted in calling " Sister Nutmeg-Grater." Mrs. Swift was a tall, wiry angular person, who seemed made of equal parts of iron and whalebone. She was never tired ; she could lift anybody, do anything ; and for sleep she seemed to have a sort of antipathy, preferring to sit in an easy-chair and drop off into little dozes, whenever it was convenient, to going regularly to bed for a night's rest.

Amy took to her from the first, and the new nurse managed her beautifully. No one else could soothe her half so well during the delirious period, when the little shrill voice seemed never to be still, and went on all day and all night in alternative raving or screaming, or, what was saddest of all to hear, low pitiful moans. There was no shutting in these sounds. People moved out of the rooms below and on either side, because they could get no sleep; and till the arrival of Nurse Swift, there was no rest for poor Mrs. Ashe, who could not keep away from her darling for a moment while that mournful wailing sounded in her ears.

Somehow the long, dry Englishwoman seemed to have a mesmeric effect on Amy, who was never quite so violent after she arrived. Katy was more thankful for this than can well be told; for her great underlying dread—a dread she dared not whisper plainly even to herself—was that " Polly dear " might break down before Amy was better, and then what *should* they do ?

She took every care that was possible of her friend. She made her eat; she made her lie down. She forced daily doses of quinine and port-wine down her throat and saved her every possible step. But no one, however affectionate and willing, could do much to lift the crushing burden of care, which was changing Mrs. Ashe's rosy fairness to wan pallor and laying such dark shadows under the pretty grey eyes. She had taken small thought of looks since Amy's illness. All the little touches which had made her toilette becoming, all the crimps and fluffs, had disappeared; yet somehow never had she seemed to Katy half so lovely as now in the plain black gown which she wore all day long, with her hair tucked into a knot behind her ears. Her real beauty of feature and outline seemed only enhanced by the rigid plainness of her attire, and the charm of true expression grew in her face. Never had Katy admired and loved her friend so well as during those days of fatigue and wearing suspense, or realised so strongly the worth of her sweetness of temper, her unselfishness and power of devoting herself to other people.

" Polly bears it wonderfully," she wrote her father, " she was all broken down for the first day or two, but now her courage and patience are surprising. When I think how precious Amy is to her, and how lonely her life would be if she were to die, I can hardly keep the tears out of my eyes. But Polly does not cry. She is quiet and brave and almost cheerful all the time, keeping herself busy with what needs to be done ; she never complains, and she looks—oh, so pretty ! I think I never knew how much she had in her before."

All this time no word had come from Lieutenant Worthington. His sister had written him as soon as Amy was taken ill, and had twice telegraphed since, but no answer had been received, and this strange silence added to the sense of lonely isolation and distance from home.

So, first one week and then another wore themselves away somehow. The fever did not break on the fourteenth day, as had been hoped, and must run for another period, the doctor said ; but its force was lessened, and he considered that a favourable sign. Amy was quieter now and did not rave so constantly, but she was very weak. All her pretty hair had been shorn away, which made her little face look tiny and sharp. Mabel's golden wig was sacrificed at the same time. Amy had insisted upon it, and they dared not cross her.

One day, Katy, coming in from a round of errands, found Mrs. Ashe standing erect and pale, with a frightened look in her eyes, and her back against Amy's door, as if defending it from somebody. Confronting her was Madame Frulini, the *padrona* of the hotel. Madame's cheeks were red, and her eyes bright and fierce ; she was evidently in a rage about something, and was pouring out a torrent of excited Italian, with now and then a French or English word slipped in by way of punctuation, and all so rapidly that only a trained ear could have followed or grasped her meaning.

" What *is* the matter ? " asked Katy in amazement.

" Oh, Katy, I am so glad you have come ! " cried poor Mrs. Ashe. " I can hardly understand a word that this horrible woman says, but I think she wants to turn us out of the hotel, and that we shall take Amy to some other place. It would be the death of her—I know it would. I never, never will go, unless the doctor says it is safe. I oughtn't to—I couldn't; she can't make me, can she, Katy?"

"Madame," said Katy—and there was a flash in her eyes before which the landlady rather shrank—"what is all this? Why do you come to trouble madame while her child is so ill?"

Then came another torrent of explanation which didn't explain; but Katy gathered enough of the meaning to make out that Mrs. Ashe was quite correct in her guess, and that Madame Frulini was requesting, nay, insisting, that they should remove Amy from the hotel at once. There was plenty of apartments to be had now that the Carnival was over, she said—her own cousin had rooms close by—it could easily be arranged, and people were going away from the Del Mondo every day because there was fever in the house. Such a thing could not be, it should not be—the landlady's voice rose to a shriek, "the child must go!"

"You are a cruel woman," said Katy indignantly, when she had grasped the meaning of the outburst. "It is wicked, it is cowardly, to come thus and attack a poor lady under your roof who has so much already to bear. It is her only child who is lying in there—her only one, do you understand, madame?— and she is a widow. What you ask might kill the child. I shall not permit you or any of your people to enter that door until the doctor comes, and then I shall tell him how you have behaved, and we shall see what he will say." As she spoke she turned the key of Amy's door, took it out and put it in her pocket, then faced the *padrona* steadily, looking her straight in the eyes.

"Mademoiselle," stormed the landlady, "I give you my word, four people have left this house already because of the noises made by little miss. More will go. I shall lose my winter's profit—all of it—all; it will be said there is fever at the Del Mondo—no one will hereafter come to me. There are lodgings plenty, comfortable—oh, so comfortable! I will not have my season ruined by a sickness; no, I will not!"

Madame Frulini's voice was again rising to a scream.

"Be silent!" said Katy sternly; "you will frighten the child. I am sorry that you should lose any customers, madame, but the fever is here and we are here, and here we must stay till it is safe to go. The child shall not be moved till the doctor gives permission. Money is not the only thing in the world ! Mrs. Ashe will pay anything that is fair to make up your losses to you, but you must leave this room now, and not return till Dr. Hilary is here."

Where Katy found French for all these long coherent speeches, she could never afterwards imagine. She tried to explain it by saying that excitement inspired her for the moment, but that as soon as the moment was over the inspiration died away and left her as speechless and confused as ever. Clover said it made her think of the miracle of Balaam ; and Katy merrily rejoined that it might be so, and that no donkey in any age of the world could possibly have been more grateful than was she for the sudden gift of speech.

" But it is not the money—it is my prestige," declared the landlady.

" Thank heaven ! Here is the doctor now," cried Mrs. Ashe.

The doctor had, in fact, been standing in the doorway for several moments before they noticed him, and had overheard part of the colloquy with Madame Frulini. With him was someone else, at the sight of whom Mrs. Ashe gave a great sob of relief. It was her brother at last.

When Italian meets Italian then comes the tug of expletive. In five minutes Madame Frulini was, metaphorically speaking, on her knees, and the doctor standing over her with drawn sword, making her take back every word she had said and every threat she had uttered.

" Prestige of thy miserable hotel ! " he thundered ; " where will that be when I go and tell the English and Americans—all of whom I know, every one !—how thou hast served a country-woman of theirs in thy house ! Dost thou think thy prestige will help thee much when Dr. Hilary has fixed a black mark on thy door ? I tell thee no ; not a stranger shalt thou have next year to eat so much as a plate of macaroni under thy base roof ! I will advertise thy behaviour in all the foreign papers—in *Figaro*, in *Galignani*, in the *Swiss Times*, and the English one which is read by all the nobility, and the *Heraldo* of New York, which all Americans peruse——"

" Oh, doctor—pardon me—I regret what I said—I am afflicted——! "

Having thus reduced Madame Frulini to powder, the doctor now condescended to take breath and listen to her appeals for mercy; and presently he brought her in with her mouth full of protestations and apologies, and assurances that the ladies had mistaken her meaning, she had only spoken for the good of all; nothing was farther from her intention than that they should be disturbed or offended in any way, and she and all her household were at the service of " the little sick angel of God." After which the doctor dismissed her with an air of contemptuous tolerance, and laid his hand on the door of Amy's room. Behold, it was locked!

" Oh, I forgot ! " cried Katy, laughing, and she pulled the key out of her pocket.

" You are a hee-roine, madcmoiselle," said Dr. Hilary. " I watched you as you faced that tigress, and your eyes were like a swordsman's as he regards his enemy's rapier."

" Oh, she was so brave, and such a help ! " said Mrs. Ashe, kissing her impulsively. " You can't think how she has stood by me all through, Ned, or what a comfort she has been."

" Yes, I can," said Ned Worthington, with a warm, grateful look at Katy. " I can believe anything good of Miss Carr."

" But where have *you* been all this time ! " said Katy, who felt this flood of compliments to be embarrassing; " we have so wondered at not hearing from you."

" I have been off on a ten-days' leave to Corsica for moufflon-shooting," replied Mr. Worthington. "I only got Polly's telegrams and letters the day before yesterday, and I came away as soon as I could get my leave extended. It was a most unlucky absence. I shall always regret it."

" Oh, it is all right now that you have come ! " his sister said, leaning her head on his arm with a look of relief and rest which was good to see. " Everything will go better now, I am sure."

" Katy Carr has behaved like a perfect angel," she told her brother when they were alone.

" She is a trump of a girl. I came in time for part of that scene with the landlady, and upon my word she was glorious ! I didn't suppose she could look so handsome."

" Have the Pages left Nice yet ? " asked his sister, rather irrelevantly.

" No—at least they were there on Thursday, but I think that they were to start to-day."

Mr. Worthington answered carelessly, but his face darkened as he spoke. There had been a little scene in Nice which he could not forget. He was sitting in the English garden with Lilly and her mother when his sister's telegrams were brought to him ; and he had read them aloud, partly as an explanation for the immediate departure which they made necessary and which broke up an excursion just arranged with the ladies for the afternoon. It is not pleasant to have plans interfered with ; and as neither Mrs. Page nor her daughter cared personally for little Amy, it is not strange that disappointment at the interruption of their pleasure should have been the first impulse with them. Still, this did not excuse Lilly's unstudied exclamation of " Oh, bother ! " and though she speedily repented it as an indiscretion, and was properly sympathetic, and " hoped the poor little thing would soon be better," Amy's uncle could not forget the jarring impression. It completed a process of disenchantment which had long been going on ; and as hearts are sometimes caught at the rebound, Mrs. Ashe was not so far astray when she built certain little dim sisterly hopes on his evident admiration for Katy's courage and this sudden awakening to a sense of her good looks.

But no space was left for sentimental match-making while still Amy's fate hung in the balance, and all three of them found plenty to do during the next fortnight. The fever did not turn on the twenty-first day, and another weary week of suspense set in, each day bringing a decrease of the dangerous symptoms, but each day as well marking a lessening in the childish strength which had been so long and severely tested. Amy was quite conscious now, and lay quietly, sleeping a great deal and speaking seldom. There was not much to do but to wait and hope ; but the flame of hope burned low at times, as the little life flickered in its socket, and seemed likely to go out like a wind-blown torch.

Now and then Lieutenant Worthington would persuade his sister to go with him for a few minutes' drive or walk in the fresh air, from which she had so long been debarred, and once or twice he prevailed on Katy to do the same ; but neither of them could bear to be away long from Amy's bedside.

Intimacy grows fast when people are thus united by a common anxiety, sharing the same hopes and fears day after day, speaking and thinking of the same thing. The gay young officer at Nice, who had counted so little in Katy's world, seemed to have disappeared, and the gentle, considerate, tender-hearted fellow who now filled his place was quite a different person in her eyes. Katy began to count on Ned Worthington as a friend who could be trusted for help and sympathy and comprehension, and appealed to and relied upon in all emergencies. She was quite at ease with him now, and asked him to do this and that, to come and help her, or to absent himself, as freely as if he had been Dorry or Phil.

He, on his part, found this easy intimacy charming. In the reaction of his temporary glamour for the pretty Lilly, Katy's very difference from her was an added attraction. This difference consisted, as much as anything else, in the fact that she was so truly in earnest in what she said and did. Had Lilly been in Katy's place, she would probably have been helpful to Mrs. Ashe and kind to Amy so far as in her lay; but the thought of self would have tinctured all that she did and said, and the need of keeping to what was tasteful and becoming would have influenced her in every emergency, and never have been absent from her mind.

Katy, on the contrary, absorbed in the needs of the moment, gave little heed to how she looked or what anyone was thinking about her. Her habit of neatness made her take time for the one thorough daily dressing—the brushing of hair and refreshing of clothes which were customary with her ; but, this tax paid to personal comfort, she gave little further heed to appearances. She wore an old grey gown, day in and day out, which Lilly would not have put on for half an hour without a large bribe, so unbecoming was it ; but somehow Lieutenant Worthington grew to like the grey gown as a part of Katy herself.

The grey gown played its part during the long, anxious night when they all sat watching breathlessly to see which way the tide would turn with dear little Amy. The doctor came at midnight, and went away to come again at dawn. Mrs. Swift sat

grim and watchful beside the pillow of her charge, rising now
and then to feel pulse and skin, or to put a spoonful of something between Amy's lips. The doors and windows stood open
to admit the air. In the outer room all was hushed. A dim
Roman lamp, fed with olive-oil, burned in one corner behind a
screen. Mrs. Ashe lay on the sofa with her eyes closed, bearing
the strain of suspense in absolute silence. Her brother sat
beside her, holding in his one of the hot hands whose nervous
twitches alone told of the surgings of hope and fear within.
Katy was resting in a big chair near by, her wistful eyes fixed on
Amy's little figure seen in the dim distance, her ears alert for
every sound from the sick-room.

A faint stir of wind and a little broadening of the light
roused Katy from a trance of half-understood thoughts. She
crept once more into Amy's room. Mrs. Swift laid a warning
finger on her lips ; Amy was sleeping, she said with a gesture.
Katy whispered the news to the still figure on the sofa, then she
went noiselessly out of the room. The great hotel was fast
asleep ; not a sound stirred the profound silence of the dark
halls. A longing for fresh air led her to the roof.

There was the dawn just tinging the east. The sky, even thus
early, wore the deep, mysterious blue of Italy. A fresh *tramon-
tana* was blowing, and made Katy glad to draw her shawl about
her.

Faint rumblings of wheels and here and there a curl of smoke,
showed that Rome was waking up. The light insensibly grew
upon the darkness. A pink flush lit up the horizon.

A footstep startled her. Ned Worthington was coming over
the roof on tiptoe, as if fearful of disturbing somebody. His
face looked resolute and excited.

" I wanted to tell you," he said in a hushed voice, " that the
doctor is here, and he says Amy has no fever, and with care
may be considered out of danger."

" Thank God ! " cried Katy, bursting into tears. The long
fatigue, the fears kept in check so resolutely, the sleepless night
just passed, had their revenge now, and she cried and cried as
if she could never stop, but with all the time such joy and
gratitude in her heart ! She was conscious that Ned had his
arm round her and was holding both her hands tight ; but they

were so one in the emotion of the moment that it did not seem strange.

"How sweet the sun looks!" she said presently, releasing herself, with a happy smile flashing through her tears; "it hasn't seemed really bright for ever so long. How silly I was to cry! Where is dear Polly? I must go down to her at once. Oh, what does she say?"

CHAPTER XI

NEXT

LIEUTENANT WORTHINGTON'S leave had nearly expired. He must rejoin his ship; but he waited till the last possible moment in order to help his sister through the move to Albano, where it had been decided that Amy should go for a few days of hill air before undertaking the longer journey to Florence.

It was a perfect morning in late March when the pale little invalid was carried in her uncle's strong arms, and placed in the carriage which was to take them to the old town on the mountain slopes which they had seen shining from far away for so many weeks past. Spring had come in her fairest shape to Italy.

When once the Campagna with its long line of aqueducts, arches, and hoary tombs, was left behind, and the carriage slowly began to mount the gradual rises of the hill, Amy revived. With every breath of the fresher air her eyes seemed to brighten and her voice to grow stronger. She held Mabel up to look at the view; and the sound of her laugh, faint and feeble as it was, was like music to her mother's ears.

Amy wore a droll little silk-lined cap on her head, under which a downy growth of pale-brown fuzz was gradually thickening. Already it showed a tendency to form into tiny rings, which to Amy, who had always hankered for curls, was an extreme satisfaction. Strange to say, the same thing exactly had happened to Mabel; her hair had grown out into soft little round curls also; Uncle Ned and Katy had ransacked Rome for this baby-wig, which filled and realised all Amy's hopes for her child. On the same excursion they had bought the materials for the pretty spring suit which Mabel wore, for it had been deemed necessary to sacrifice most of her wardrobe as a concession to possible fever-germs. Amy admired the pearl-coloured dress and hat, the fringed jacket and little lace-trimmed parasol, so much that she was quite consoled for the loss of the blue velvet costume and ermine muff which had been the pride of her heart ever since they left Paris, and whose destruction they had scarcely dared to confess to her.

So up, up, up they climbed till the gateway of the old town was passed, and the carriage stopped before a quaint building, once the residence of the Bishop of Albano, but now known as the Hôtel de la Poste. Here they alighted, and were shown up a wide and lofty staircase to their rooms.

Such enormous rooms as they were ! It was quite a journey to go from one side of them to another. The floors were of stone, with squares of carpet laid down over them, which looked absurdly small for the great spaces they were supposed to cover. The beds and tables were of the usual size, but they seemed almost doll furniture because the chambers were so big. A quaint old paper, with an enormous pattern of banyan-trees and pagodas, covered the walls, and every now and then betrayed, by an oblong of regular cracks, the existence of a hidden door, papered to look exactly like the rest of the wall.

These mysterious doors made Katy nervous, and she never rested till she had opened every one of them and explored the places they led to. One gave access to a queer little bathroom. Another led, through a narrow dark passage, to a sort of balcony or loggia overhanging the garden. A third ended in a dusty closet with an artful chink in it from which you could peep into what had been the bishop's drawing-room, but which was now turned into the dining-room of the hotel. It seemed made for purposes of espial; and Katy had visions of a long line of reverend prelates with their ears glued to the chink, overhearing what was being said about them in the apartment beyond.

Before he left them Lieutenant Worthington had a talk with his sister in the garden. She rather forced this talk upon him, for various things were lying at her heart about which she

longed for explanation; but he yielded so easily to her wiles
that it was evident he was not averse to the idea.

"Come, Polly, don't beat about the bush any longer," he said
at last, amused and a little irritated at her half-hints and little
feminine *finesses*. "I know what you want to ask; and as there's
no use making a secret of it, I will take my turn in asking. Have
I any chance, do you think?"

"Any chance!—about Katy, do you mean? Oh, Ned, you
make me so happy!"

"Yes; about her, of course."

"I don't see why you should say 'of course'," remarked his
sister, with the perversity of her sex, "when it's only five or
six weeks ago that I was lying awake at night for fear you were
being gobbled up by that Lilly Page."

"There was little risk of it," replied her brother seriously.
"She's awfully pretty and she dances beautifully, and the other
fellows were all wild about her, and—well, you know yourself
how such things go. I can't see now what it was that I fancied
so much about her. I don't suppose I could have told exactly at
the time; but I can tell without the smallest trouble what it is in
—the other."

"In Katy? I should think so," cried Mrs. Ashe emphatic-
ally; "the two are no more to be compared than—than—well,
bread and syllabub! You can live on one and you can't live on
the other."

"Come now, Miss Page isn't so bad as that. She is a nice
girl enough, and a pretty girl, too,—prettier than Katy; I'm
not so far gone that I can't see that. But we won't talk about her,
she's not in the present question at all; very likely she'd have
had nothing to say to me in any case. I was only one out of a
dozen, and she never gave me reason to suppose that she cared
more for me than the rest. Let us talk about this friend of
yours; have I any chance at all, do you think, Polly?"

"Ned, you are the dearest boy! I would rather have Katy for
a sister than anyone else I know. She's so nice all through—so
true and sweet and satisfactory."

"She is all that and more; she's a woman to tie to for life, to
be perfectly sure of always. She would make a splendid wife
for any man. I'm not half good enough for her; but the

question is—and you haven't answered it yet, Polly—what's my chance?"

"I don't know," said his sister slowly.

"Then I must ask her; and I shall do so to-day."

"I don't know," repeated Mrs. Ashe. "'She is a woman, therefore to be won': and I don't think there is anyone ahead of you; that is the best hope I have to offer, Ned. Katy never talks of such things; and though she's so frank, I can't guess whether or not she ever thinks about them. She likes you, however, I am sure of that. But, Ned, it will not be wise to say anything to her yet."

"Not say anything! Why not?"

"No. Recollect that it is only a little while since she looked upon you as the admirer of another girl, and a girl she doesn't like very much, though they are cousins. You must give her time to get over that impression. Wait a while, that's my advice, Ned."

"I'll wait any time if only she will say yes in the end. But it's hard to go away without a word of hope, and it's more like a man to speak out, it seems to me."

"It's too soon," persisted his sister. "You don't want her to think you a fickle fellow, falling in love with a fresh girl every time you go into port, and falling out again when the ship sails. Sailors have a bad reputation for that sort of thing. No woman cares to win a man like that."

"Great Scott! I should think not! Do you mean to say that is the way my conduct appears to her, Polly?"

"No, I don't mean just that; but wait, dear Ned, I am sure it is better."

Fortified by this sage counsel, Lieutenant Worthington went away next morning, without saying anything to Katy in words, though perhaps eyes and tones may have been less discreet. He made them promise that someone should send a letter every day about Amy; and as Mrs. Ashe frequently devolved the writing of these bulletins upon Katy, and the replies came in the shape of long letters, she found herself conducting a pretty regular correspondence without quite intending it. Ned Worthington wrote particularly nice letters. He had the knack, more often found in women than men, of giving a picture with

a few graphic touches and indicating what was droll or what was
characteristic with a single happy phrase. His letters grew to
be one of Katy's pleasures; and sometimes, as Mrs. Ashe
watched the colour deepen in her cheeks while she read, her
heart would bound hopefully within her. But she was a wise
woman in her way, and she wanted Katy for a sister very much;
so she never said a word or looked a look to startle or surprise
her, but left the thing to work itself out, which is the best course
always in love affairs.

Little Amy's improvement at Albano was something remarkable. Mrs. Swift watched over her like a lynx. Her
vigilance never relaxed. Amy was made to eat and sleep and
walk and rest with the regularity of a machine; and this exact
system, combined with the good air, worked like a charm. The
little one gained hour by hour. They could absolutely see her
growing fat, her mother declared.

She had gained so much before the time came to start for
Florence that they scarcely dreaded the journey; but it proved
worse than their expectations. They had not been able to secure
a carriage to themselves, and were obliged to share their com-
partment with two English ladies, and three Roman Catholic
priests, one old, the others young. The older priest seemed to
be a person of some consequence, for quite a number of
people came to see him off, and knelt for his blessing devoutly
as the train moved away. The younger ones Katy guessed to
be seminary students under his charge.

At last the train, steaming down the valley of the Arno,
revealed fair Florence sitting among olive-clad hills, with
Giotti's beautiful Bell-tower, and the great, many-coloured,
soft-hued Cathedral, and the square tower of the old Palace,
and the quaint bridges over the river, looking exactly as they do
in the photographs; and Katy would have felt delighted, in
spite of dust and fatigue, had not Amy looked so worn out and
exhausted. They were seriously troubled about her, and for the
moment could think of nothing else. Happily the fatigue did no
permanent harm, and a day or two of rest made her all right
again. By good fortune, a nice little apartment in the modern
quarter of the city had been vacated by its winter occupants the
very day of their arrival, and Mrs. Ashe secured it for a month,

with all its conveniences and advantages, including a maid named Maria, who had been servant to the just-departed tenants.

Maria was a very tall woman, at least six feet two, and had a splendid contralto voice, which she occasionally exercised while busy over her pots and pans. It was so remarkable to hear these grand arias and recitatives proceeding from a kitchen some eight feet square that Katy was at great pains to satisfy her curiosity about it. By aid of the dictionary and much persistent questioning, she made out that Maria in her youth had received a partial training for the opera; but in the end it was decided that she was too big and heavy for the stage, and the poor " giantess," as Amy named her, had been forced to abandon her career, and gradually had sunk to the position of maid-of-all-work. Katy suspected that heaviness of mind as well as of body must have stood in her way ; for Maria, though a good-natured giantess, was by no means quick of intelligence.

" I do think that the manner in which people over here can make homes for themselves at five minutes' notice is perfectly delightful," cried Katy, at the end of their first day's house-keeping. " I wish we could do the same in America. How cosy it looks here already ! "

It was indeed cosy. Their new domain consisted of a parlour in a corner, furnished in bright yellow brocade, with windows to south and west ; a nice little dining-room ; three bedrooms, with dimity-curtained beds ; a square entrance-hall, lighted at night by a tall slender brass lamp whose double wicks were fed with olive-oil ; and the aforesaid tiny kitchen, behind which was a sleeping-cubby, quite too small to be good fit for the giantess. The rooms were full of conveniences—easy-chairs, sofas, plenty of bureaus and dressing-tables, and corner fireplaces like Franklin stoves, in which odd little fires burned on cool days, made of pine cones, cakes of pressed sawdust exactly like Boston brown bread cut into slices, and a few sticks of wood thriftily adjusted, for fuel is worth its weight in gold in Florence. Katy's was the smallest of the bedrooms but she liked it best of all for the reason that its one big window opened on an iron balcony over which grew a Banksia rose-vine with a stem as thick as her wrist. It was covered just now with masses of tiny white blossoms, whose fragrance was inexpressibly delicious and made every breath drawn in their neighbourhood a delight. The sun streamed in on all sides of the little apartment, which filled a narrowing angle at the union of three streets ; and from one window and another, glimpses could be caught of the distant heights about the city—San Miniato in one direction, Bello Sguardo in another, and for the third the long olive-hung ascent of Fiesole, crowned by its grey cathedral towers.

It was astonishing how easily everything fell into train about this little establishment. Every morning at six the English baker left two small sweet brown loaves and a dozen rolls at the door. Then followed the dairyman with a supply of tiny leaf-shaped pats of freshly-churned butter, a big flask of milk, and two small bottles of thick cream with a twist of vine leaf in each by way of a cork. Next came a *contadino* with a flask of red Chianti wine, a film of oil floating on top to keep it sweet. People in Florence must drink wine, whether they like it or not, because the lime-impregnated water is unsafe for use without some admixture.

Dinner came from a *trattoria*, in a tin box, with a pan of coals inside to keep it warm, which box was carried on a man's head. It was furnished at a fixed price per day—a soup, two dishes of meat, two vegetables, and a sweet dish ; and the supply was so generous as always to leave something towards next day's luncheon. Salad, fruit, and fresh eggs Maria bought for them in the old market. From the confectioner's came loaves of *pane santo*, a sort of light cake made with arrow-root instead of flour ; and sometimes, by way of a treat, a square of *pan forte da Siena*, compounded of honey, almonds and chocolate—a mixture as pernicious as it is delicious, and which might take a medal anywhere for the sure production of nightmares.

Amy soon learned to know the shops from which these delicacies came. She had her favourites, too, among the strolling merchants who sold oranges and those little sweet native figs dried in the sun without sugar, which are among the specialities of Florence. They, in their turn, learned to know her and to watch for the appearance of her little capped head and Mabel's blond wig at the window, lingering about till she came, and advertising their wares with musical modulations, so appealing that Amy was always running to Katy, who acted as housekeeper to beg her to please buy this or that, " because it is my old man, and he wants me to so much."

" But, chicken, we have plenty of figs for to-day."

" No matter ; get some more, please do. I'll eat them all ; really, I will."

And Amy was as good as her word. Her convalescent appetite was something prodigious.

There was another branch of shopping in which they all took equal delight. The beauty and the cheapness of the Florence flowers are a continual surprise to a stranger. Every morning after breakfast an old man came creaking up the two long flights of stairs which led to Mrs. Ashe's apartment, tapped at the door, and, as soon as it opened, inserted a shabby elbow and a large flat basket full of flowers. Such flowers ! Great masses of scarlet and cream-coloured tulips, and white and gold narcissus, knots of roses of all shades, carnations, heavy-headed trails of wistaria, wild hyacinths, violets, deep crimson and orange ranunculus, *giglios,* or wild irises—the Florence emblem, so deeply purple as to be almost black—anemones, spring-beauties, faintly-tinted wood-blooms tied in large loose nosegays, ivy, fruit blossoms—everything that can be thought of that is fair and sweet. These enticing wares the old man would tip out on the table. Mrs. Ashe and Katy would select what they wanted, and then the process of bargaining would begin, without which no sale is complete in Italy. The old man would name an enormous price, five times as much as he hoped to get. Katy would offer a very small one, considerably less than she expected to give. The old man would dance with dismay, wring his hands, assure them that he should die of hunger, and all his family with him, if he took less than the price named ; he would then come down half a franc in his demand. So it would go on for five minutes, ten, sometimes for a quarter of an hour, the old man's price gradually descending, and Katy's terms very slowly going up, a cent or two at a time. Next the giantess would mingle with the fray. She would bounce out of her kitchen, berate the flower-vendor, snatch up his flowers, declare that they smelt badly, fling them down again, pouring out all the while a voluble tirade of reproaches and revilings, and looking so enormous in her excitement that Katy wondered that the old man dared to answer her at all. Finally, there would be a sudden lull. The old man would shrug his shoulders, and, remarking that he and his wife and his aged grandmother must go without bread that day since it was the signora's will, take the money offered and depart, leaving such a mass of flowers behind him that Katy would begin to think that they had paid an unfair price for them and to feel a little rueful, till she observed that the old man was absolutely dancing downstairs with rapture over the good bargain he had made, and that Maria was black with indignation over the extravagance of her ladies !

"The Americani are a nation of spendthrifts," she would mutter to herself, as she quickened the charcoal in her droll little range by fanning it with a palm-leaf fan ; "they squander money like water. Well, all the better for us Italians !" with a shrug of her shoulders.

"But, Maria, it was only sixteen cents that we paid, and look at those flowers ! There are at least half a bushel of them."

"Sixteen cents for garbage like that ! The signorina would better let me make her bargains for her. *Già ! Già !* No Italian lady would have paid more than eleven sous for such useless *roba*. It is evident that the signorina's countrymen eat gold when at home, they think so little of casting it away !"

Altogether, what with the comfort and quiet of this little home, the numberless delightful things that there were to do and to see, and Viessieux's great library, from which they could draw books at will to make the doing and seeing more intelligible, the month at Florence passed only too quickly, and was one of the times to which they afterwards looked back with most pleasure. Amy grew steadily stronger, and the freedom from anxiety about her after their long strain of apprehension was restful and healing beyond expression to both mind and body.

Their very last excursion of all, and one of the pleasantest, was to the old amphitheatre at Fiesole, and it was while they sat there in the soft glow of the late afternoon, tying into bunches the violets which they had gathered from under walls whose foundations antedate Rome itself, that a cheery call sounded from above, and an unexpected suprise descended upon them in the shape of Lieutenant Worthington, who, having secured another fifteen days' furlough, had come to take his sister on to Venice.

"I didn't write you that I had applied for leave," he explained, "because there seemed so little chance of me getting off again so soon; but as luck had it, Carruthers, whose turn it was, sprained his ankle and was laid up, and the Commodore let us exchange. I made all the capital I could out of Amy's fever; but upon my word, I felt like a humbug when I came upon her and Mrs. Swift in the Cascine just now, as I was hunting for you. How she has picked up! I should never have known her for the same child."

"Yes, she seems perfectly well again, and as strong as before she had the fever, though that dear old Goody Swift is just as careful of her as ever. She would not let us bring her here this afternoon, for fear we should stay out till the dew fell. Ned, it is perfectly delightful that you were able to come. It makes going to Venice seem quite a different thing, doesn't it, Katy?"

"I don't want it to seem quite different, because going to Venice was always one of my dreams," replied Katy, with a little laugh.

"I hope at least it doesn't make it seem less pleasant," said Mr. Worthington, as his sister stopped to pick a violet.

"No, indeed, I am glad," said Katy; "we shall all be seeing it for the first time, too, shall we not? I think you said you had never been there." She spoke simply and frankly, but she was conscious of an odd shyness.

"I simply couldn't stand it any longer," Ned Worthington confided to his sister when they were alone. "My head is so full of her that I can't attend to my work, and it came to me all of a sudden that this might be my last chance. You'll be going north before long, you know, to Switzerland and so on, where I cannot follow you. So I made a clean breast of it to the Commodore; and the good old fellow, who has a soft spot in his heart for a love-story, behaved like a brick, and made it all straight for me to come away."

Mrs. Ashe did not join in these commendations of the Commodore; her attention was fixed on another part of her brother's discourse.

" Then you won't be able to come to me again ? I shan't see you again after this ! '' she exclaimed. " Dear me ! I never realised that before. What shall I do without you ? "

" You will have Miss Carr. She is a host in herself," suggested Ned Worthington. His sister shook her head.

" Katy is a jewel," she remarked presently ; " but somehow one wants a man to call upon. I shall feel lost without you, Ned."

The month's housekeeping wound up that night with a " thick tea " in honour of Lieutenant Worthington's arrival, which taxed all the resources of the little establishment. Maria was sent out hastily to buy *pan forte da Siena* and *vino d'Asti*, and fresh eggs for an omelette, and chickens' breasts smothered in cream from the restaurant, and artichokes for a salad, and flowers to garnish all ; and the guest ate and praised and admired ; and Amy and Mabel sat on his knee and explained everything to him, and they were all very happy together. Their merriment was so infectious that it extended to the poor giantess, who had been very pensive all day at the prospect of losing her good place, and who now raised her voice in the grand aria from " Orfeo," and made the kitchen ring with the passionate demand " *Che fara senza Eurydice ?* " The splendid notes, full of fire and lamentation, rang out across the saucepans as effectively as if they had been footlights ; and Katy, rising softly, opened the kitchen door a little way that they might not lose a sound.

The next day brought them to Venice. It was a " moment," indeed, as Katy seated herself for the first time in a gondola, and looked from beneath its black hood at the palace walls on the Grand Canal, past which they were gliding. Some were creamy white and black, some orange-tawny, others of a dull delicious ruddy colour, half-pink, half-red ; but all, in build and ornament, were unlike palaces elsewhere. High on the prow before her stood the gondolier, his form defined in dark outline against the sky, as he swayed and bent to his long oar, raising his head now and again to give a wild musical cry, as warning to other approaching gondolas. It was all like a dream. Ned Worthington sat beside her, looking more at the changes in her expressive face than at the palaces. Venice was as new to him as to Katy ; but she was a new feature in his life also, and even more interesting than Venice.

They seemed to float on pleasures for the next ten days. Their arrival had been happily timed to coincide with a great popular festival which for nearly a week kept Venice in a state of continual brilliant gala. All the days were spent on the water, only landing now and then to look at some famous building or picture, or to eat ices in the Piazza with the lovely façade of St. Mark's before them. Dining or sleeping seemed a sheer waste of time ! The evenings were spent on the water too ; for every night, immediately after sunset, a beautiful drifting pageant started from the front of the Doge's Palace to make the tour of the Grand Canal, and our friends always took a part in it. In its centre went a barge hung with embroideries and filled with orange-trees and musicians. This was surrounded by a great convoy of skiffs and gondolas bearing coloured lanterns and pennons and gay awnings, and managed by gondoliers in picturesque uniforms. All these floated and shifted and swept on together with a sort of rhythmic undulations, as if keeping time to the music, while across their path dazzling showers and arches of coloured fire poured from the palace fronts and the hotels. Every movement of the fairy flotilla was repeated in the illuminated water, every torch-tip and scarlet lantern and flake of green or rosy fire, above all the bright full moon looked down as if surprised. It was magically beautiful in effect. Katy felt as if her previous sober ideas about life and things had melted away. For the moment the world was turned topsy-turvy. There was nothing hard or real or sordid left in it ; it was just a fairy tale, and she was in the middle of it as she had longed to be in her childhood. She was the Princess, encircled by delights, as when she and Clover and Elsie played in " Paradise "—only this was better ; and, dear me, who was this Prince who seemed to belong to the story and to grow more important to it every day ?

Fairy tales must come to ending. Katy's last chapter closed with a sudden turn-over of the leaf when, towards the end of this happy fortnight, Mrs. Ashe came into her room with the face of one who has unpleasant news to communicate.

" Katy," she began, " should you be *awfully* disappointed,

should you consider me a perfect wretch, if I went home now instead of in the autumn ? "

Katy was too much astonished to reply.

" I am grown such a coward, I am so knocked up and weakened by what I suffered in Rome, that I find I cannot face the idea of going on to Germany and Switzerland alone, without Ned to take care of me. You are a perfect angel, dear, and I know that you would do all you could to make it easy for me, but I am such a fool that I do not dare. I think my nerves must have given way," she continued half-tearfully ; " but the very idea of shifting for myself for five months longer makes me so miserably homesick that I cannot endure it. I dare say I shall repent afterwards, and I tell myself now how silly it is, but it's no use—I shall never know another easy moment till I have Amy safe again in America and under your father's care.

" I find," she continued, after another little pause, " that we can go down with Ned to Genoa and take a steamer there which will carry us straight to New York without any stops. I hate to disappoint you dreadfully, Katy, but I have almost decided to do it. Shall you mind very much ? Can you ever forgive me ? " She was fairly crying now.

Katy had to swallow hard before she could answer, the sense of disappointment was so sharp ; and with all her efforts there was almost a sob in her voice as she said :

" Why, yes, indeed, dear Polly, there is nothing to forgive. You are perfectly right to go home if you feel so." Then with another swallow she added : " You have given me the loveliest six months' treat that ever was, and I should be a greedy girl indeed if I found fault because it is cut off a little sooner than we expected."

" You are so dear and good not to be vexed," said her friend, embracing her. " It makes me feel doubly sorry about disappointing you. Indeed I wouldn't if I could help it, but I simply can't. I *must* go home. Perhaps we'll come back some day when Amy is grown up, or safely married to somebody who will take good care of her ! "

This distant prospect was but a poor consolation for the immediate disappointment. The more Katy thought about it the sorrier did she feel. It was not only losing the chance—very

likely the only one she would ever have—of seeing Switzerland
and Germany; it was all sorts of other little things besides.
They must go home in a strange ship with a captain they did
not know, instead of in the *Spartacus*, as they had planned,
and they should land in New York, where no one would be
waiting for them, and not have the fun of sailing into Boston
Bay and seeing Rose on the wharf, where she had promised to
be. Furthermore, they must pass the hot summer in Burnet
instead of in the cool Alpine valleys; and Polly's house was let
till October. She and Amy would have to shift for themselves
elsewhere. Perhaps they would not be in Burnet at all. Oh dear,
what a pity it was, what a dreadful pity!

Then, the first shock of surprise and discomfiture over, other
ideas asserted themselves; and as she realised that in three
weeks more, or four at the longest, she was to see papa and
Clover and all her dear people at home, she began to feel so very
glad that she could hardly wait for the time to come. After all
there was nothing in Europe quite so good as that.

" No, I'm not sorry," she told herself; " I am glad. Poor
Polly! It's no wonder she feels nervous after all she has gone
through. I hope I wasn't cross to her! And it will be *very* nice
to have Lieutenant Worthington to take care of us as far as
Genoa."

The next three days were full of work. There was no more
floating in gondolas, except in the way of business. All the
shopping which they had put off must be done, and the trunks
packed for the voyage. Everyone recollected last errands and
commissions; there was continual coming and going and confusion. And Amy, wild with excitement, popping up every
other moment in the midst of it all, to demand of everybody if
they were not glad that they were going back to America.

Katy had never yet bought her gift for old Mrs. Redding.
She had waited, thinking continually that she should see something more tempting still in the next place they went to; but
now, with the sense that there were to be no more " next
places," she resolved to wait no longer, and with a hundred
francs in her pocket, set forth to choose something from among
the many tempting things for sale in the Piazza. A bracelet of
old Roman coins had caught her fancy one day in a bric-à-brac

shop and she walked straight towards it, only pausing by the way to buy a pale-blue iridescent pitcher at Salviate's for Cecy Slack, and see it carefully rolled in sea-weed and soft paper.

The price of the bracelet was a little more than she expected, and quite a long process of bargaining was necessary to reduce it to the sum she had to spend. She had just succeeded, and was counting out the money, when Mrs. Ashe and her brother appeared, having spied her from the opposite side of the Piazza, where they were choosing last photographs at Naga's. Katy showed her purchase and explained that it was a present " for of course I should never walk out in cold blood and buy a bracelet for myself," she said, with a laugh.

" This is a fascinating little shop," said Mrs. Ashe. " I wonder what is the price of that queer old châtelaine with the bottles hanging from it."

The price was high ; but Mrs. Ashe was now tolerably conversant with shopping Italian, which consists chiefly of a few words repeated many times over, and it lowered rapidly under the influence of her *troppo*'s and *è molto caro*'s, accompanied with telling little shrugs and looks of surprise. In the end she bought it for less than two-thirds of what had been originally asked for it. As she put the parcel in her pocket, her brother said :

" If you have done your shopping now, Polly, can't you come out for a last row ? "

" Katy may, but I can't," replied Mrs. Ashe. " The man promised to bring my gloves at six o'clock, and I must be there to pay for them. Take her down to the Lido, Ned. It's an exquisite evening for the water, and the sunset promises to be delicious. You can take the time, can't you, Katy ? "

Katy could.

Mrs. Ashe turned to leave them, but suddenly stopped short.

" Katy, look ! Isn't that a picture ? "

The " picture " was Amy, who had come to the Piazza with Mrs. Swift, to feed the doves of St. Mark's, which was one of her favourite amusements. These pretty birds are the pets of all Venice, and so accustomed to being fondled and made much of by strangers that they are perfectly tame. Amy, when her mother caught sight of her, was sitting on the marble pavement, with one on her shoulder, two perched on the edge of her lap, which was full of crumbs, and a flight of others circling round her head. She was looking up and calling them in soft tones. The sunlight caught the little downy curls on her head and made them glitter. The flying doves lit on the pavement, and crowded round her, their pearl and grey and rose-tinted and white feathers, their scarlet feet and gold-ringed eyes, making a shifting confusion of colours, as they hopped and fluttered and cooed about the little maid, unstartled even by her clear laughter. Close by stood Nurse Swift, observant and grimly pleased.

The mother looked on with happy tears in her eyes. " Oh, Katy, think what she was a few weeks ago, and look at her now ! Can I ever be thankful enough ? "

She squeezed Katy's hand convulsively and walked away, turning her head now and then for another glance at Amy and the doves ; while Ned and Katy silently crossed to the landing and got into a gondola. It was the perfection of a Venice evening, with silver waves lapsing and lulling under a rose and opal sky, and the sense that it was their last row on those enchanted waters made every moment seem doubly precious.

I cannot tell you exactly what it was that Ned Worthington said to Katy during that row, or why it took so long to say it that they did not get in till after the sun was set, and the stars had come out to peep at their bright, glinting faces reflected in the Grand Canal. In fact, no one can tell ; for no one overheard, except Giacomo, the brown yellow-jacketed gondolier, and as he did not understand a word of English he could not repeat the conversation. Venetian boatmen, however, know pretty well what it means when a gentleman and lady, both young, find so much to say in low tones to each other under the gondola hood, and are so long about giving the order to return ; and Giacomo deeply sympathetic, rowed as softly and made himself as imperceptible as he could—a display of tact which merited the big silver piece with which Lieutenant Worthington " crossed his palm " on landing.

Mrs. Ashe had begun to look for them long before they appeared, but I think she was neither surprised nor sorry that they were so late. Katy kissed her hastily and went away at once—" to pack," she said—and Ned was equally undemonstrative; but they looked so happy, both of them, that " Polly dear " was quite satisfied and asked no questions.

Five days later the parting came, when the *Florio* steamer put into the port of Genoa for passengers. It was not an easy goodbye to say. Mrs. Ashe and Amy both cried, and Mabel was said to be in deep affliction also. But there were alleviations. The squadron was coming home in the autumn, and the officers would have leave to see their friends, and of course Lieutenant Worthington must come to Burnet—to visit his sister. Five months would soon go, he declared; but, for all the cheerful assurance, his face was rueful enough as he held Katy's hand in a long tight clasp while the little boat waited to take him ashore.

After that it was just waiting to be got through with till they sighted Sandy Hook and the Neversinks—a waiting varied with peeps at Marseilles and Gibraltar, and the sight of a whale or two and one distant iceberg. The weather was fair all the way, and the ocean smooth. Amy was never weary of lamenting her own stupidity in not having taken Marian Matilda out of confinement before they left Venice.

" That child has hardly been out of the trunk since we started," she said. " She hasn't seen anything except a little bit of Nice. I shall really be ashamed when the other children ask her about it. I think I shall play that she was left at boarding-school and didn't come to Europe at all! Don't you think that would be the best way, Mamma ? "

" You might play that she was left in the State prison for having done something naughty," suggested Katy; but Amy scouted this idea.

" She never does naughty things," she said, " because she never does anything at all. She's just stupid, poor child! It's not her fault."

The thirty-six hours between New York and Burnet seemed longer than all the rest of the journey put together, Katy thought. But they ended at last, as the *Lake Queen* swung to her moorings at the familiar wharf, where Dr. Carr stood surrounded with all his boys and girls just as they had stood the previous October, only that now there were no clouds on anybody's face, and Johnnie was skipping up and down for joy instead of grief. It was a long moment while the plank was being lowered from the gangway ; but the moment it was in place, Katy darted across, first ashore of all the passengers, and was in her father's arms.

Mrs. Ashe and Amy spent two or three days with them, while looking up temporary quarters elsewhere ; and so long as they stayed all seemed a happy confusion of talking and embracing and exclaiming, and distributing of gifts. After they went away things fell into their customary train, and a certain flatness became apparent. Everything had happened that could happen. The long-talked-of European journey was over. Here was Katy at home again, months sooner than they expected ; yet she looked remarkably cheerful and content ! Clover could not understand it : she was likewise puzzled to account for one or two private conversations between Katy and papa in which she had not been invited to take part, and the occasional arrival of a letter from " foreign parts " about whose contents nothing was said.

" It seems a dreadful pity that you had to come so soon," she said one day when they were alone in their bedroom. " It's delightful to have you, of course ; but we had braced ourselves to do without you till October, and there are such lots of delightful things that you could have been doing and seeing at this moment."

" Oh, yes indeed ! " replied Katy, but not at all as if she were particularly disappointed.

" Katy Carr, I don't understand you," persisted Clover. " Why don't you feel worse about it ? Here you have lost five months of the most splendid time you ever had, and you don't seem to mind it a bit ! Why, if I were in your place my heart would be perfectly broken. And you needn't have come, either ; that's the worst of it. It was just a whim of Polly's. Papa says Amy might have stayed as well as not. Why aren't you sorrier, Katy ? "

" Oh, I don't know ! Perhaps because I had so much as it was—enough to last all my life, I think, though I *should* like to go again. You can't imagine what beautiful pictures are put away in my memory."

"I don't see that you had so awfully much," said the aggravated Clover; "you were there only a little more than six months—for I don't count the sea—and ever so much of that time was taken up with nursing Amy. You can't have any pleasant pictures of *that* part of it."

"Yes, I have, some."

"Well, I should really like to know what. There you were in a dark room, frightened to death and tired to death, with only Mrs. Ashe and the old nurse to keep you company—Oh yes, that brother was there part of the time! I forgot him——"

Clover stopped short in sudden amazement. Katy was standing with her back towards her, smoothing her hair, but her face was reflected in the glass. At Clover's words a sudden deep flush had mounted in Katy's cheeks. Deeper and deeper it burned as she became conscious of Clover's astonished gaze, till even the back of her neck was pink. Then, as if she could not bear it any longer, she put the brush down, turned, and fled out of the room; while Clover, looking after her, exclaimed in a tone of sudden comical dismay :

"What does it mean? Oh, dear me! Is *that* what Katy is going to do next?"